No Surrender

The story, all names, characters, and incidents portrayed in this production are fictitious. No identification with actual persons (living or deceased), places, buildings, and products is intended or should be inferred.

Book Cover by Staci Brillhart.

Illustrations by M. DaSilva

2nd edition, 2024

Trigger and Content Warnings

MC with social anxiety, references to gun violence, the death of a sibling and being raised in the foster care system. This book also contains three very explicit intimate scenes and several instances of what could be considered foul language throughout.

Contents

Chapter 1

Sarah

I USED TO THRIVE in the spotlight. Okay, maybe not thrive. But at least I survived its glare. Because once upon a time being in the spotlight had a certain appeal. I didn't really have a choice since I practically lived there, but I made my peace with it. When I kicked the winning goal or made an amazing save it was a shot of adrenaline to bask in the attention I received.

I had no reason to believe things would change so drastically. I did all the things I was supposed to. I kept my head down and followed all the rules. All through high school and college, I made sure I brought home decent grades. I gave one hundred and ten percent on the athletic field. I quietly thrived on routine and predictability and dreamed about a different future. One where things were more exciting, and I would be surrounded by people who just got me. That I would find my tribe, my forever friends, my soulmate. That my parents would finally accept me for who I was.

Instead, one minute of violence changed my world forever. That one minute robbed me of the one cheerleader I had. It robbed me of the one person that always had my back and stood up to our parents on my behalf. I learned the hard way that the world isn't a fairytale full of birds that land on your shoulders and serenade you, or charming cowboys that sweep to the rescue on a galloping white horse and carry you off into the sunset to live happily forever after. It can be full of disappointment and heartache and days of blackness you want to lose yourself in. It can be full of moments you lose that you can never get back. Moments that live in your nightmares forever.

If I hadn't been in the spotlight I might have spent my whole life suffering under the delusion that I was safe, that bad things can't happen if you pay attention and take self-defense and always remain aware of your surroundings. Because that's what the YouTube videos and the self-defense instructors and law enforcement officers tell you. But they're wrong. That wasn't enough. While I was deluding myself, the monster came out of the shadows and turned my life upside down. I know the glare of the spotlight is what brought the monster to me, like a homing beacon.

I was never quite enough for my parents. For half my life, they referred to my soccer career as an amusing hobby and kept asking when I would get serious about making meaningful contributions to the world. I'll never forget the day I proudly announced over spaghetti dinner that I was the new starting forward of the girls' soccer team. My mother replied with, "That's nice, dear. But tonight isn't about you. Beth just became a Rhodes Scholar and I think it's worth celebrating." In other words, my accomplishment paled in comparison, was barely a blip on her radar.

When I made the Olympic team, they liked to brag about my notoriety. But then my team and I didn't bring home the gold medal and they told me I was too old for something they considered a pointless endeavor. They badgered me to settle into a real career. They badgered me about becoming a brilliant scientist like my sister, Beth. There's a reason *Jacob, Have I Loved* was my favorite book growing up. Louise was the forgotten sister, the shadowy imitation of glittering perfect Caroline. I identified with Louise. I shared her guilt and her bitterness and her deep need to belong somewhere to someone.

We're told that it's okay to be different and choose the road less traveled. Making that choice has never gone well for me. Being an outcast and begging for scraps of affection from people who only notice bright and shiny things is never fun. It's isolating, and lonely. I will never beg for scraps again. I will never put myself in that position again.

Then Beth was no longer here, and everyone blamed me because I wasn't content to hide behind the cloistered walls of academia. They started pushing even harder and I felt myself crumbling beneath the onslaught of their expectations. I shrink-wrapped everything I was into a tiny package and tried to become the replacement they wanted. I thought it would assuage the guilt they were laying on my shoulders.

Until the day I realized that I shouldn't feel guilty because life happens and it's scary and unpredictable and there are things you can't control. I found myself staring into a mirror, finally seeing they would never accept me for who I was. I knew in that moment that escaping out the window was my best option. I hastily piled my truck with three boxes full of my favorite books and movies, and a single suitcase. I hit the road with only my Husky, Sasha, for company.

I drove for two days straight, catching naps in convenient rest areas, knowing that Sasha would bite the hand off any idiot dumb enough to get close enough, before I crashed on a friend's couch in St. Louis and decided to put my teaching certificate to use. I scoured job boards until I found Willow Creek High School in the middle of nowhere rural Virginia. Luckily, the school board was desperate for a high school science teacher and hired me sight unseen based on my resume.

Now I'm afraid of being around so many people at one time and I hate crowds because they fill me with this bone-deep fear. The knowledge that I'm not safe, that I can't protect anyone, not even myself, is always there. My anxiety was always manageable, until I was trapped in a situation I couldn't escape from by my choices and my circle. Now, my fear can be paralyzing, and when my panic attacks come roaring out of nowhere I feel like a dolphin stranded on a deserted beach, gasping for air.

That fear is why I'm a high school science teacher in a small town (with a guaranteed captive audience) instead of on the pitch in front of thousands of screaming fans. It's why I left behind everything familiar and worked so hard to bury myself in this small town. I know my students and I are still in danger of attack, and the fact I need to go through active shooter drills with them makes my stomach turn. But those drills are a way of life in twenty-first century America, and the kids are so nonchalant about it they don't even realize the innocence they've lost. It never ceases to amaze me that the power-hungry overlords who run our country seem more interested in regulating my body than regulating guns.

Even when I feel like the whole world is going to complete and utter shit and everyone around me seems oblivious, living in a small town is still better than living in the city. It suits me to a tee because they don't know my history. They don't have ridiculous expectations for my future. Sure, they've seen the YouTube videos and the ESPN highlights, but I'm old news because I'm retired. They only trot out my credentials to impress stuck-up parents from rival schools who talk shit about people they call hillbillies.

Here in Willow Creek, I know what to expect because I have everything planned down to the last detail. After first week jitters at the beginning of every school year, I always settle into my groove. I think about that instead of being around this many people in one place at one time. I think about that instead of my sensory overload. These days, all I want is quiet and focus and a glass of wine by myself while I watch the stars. Crowds are a freaking nightmare. They made me anxious before the pandemic, but after two years of teaching and living like a hermit, it's even worse. My nightmares torture me more than ever, and something I occasionally tolerated in the past is now something I want to avoid at all costs.

Standing here just waiting means I'm sacrificing a piece of my sanity and my skin is crawling right now, like I just saw an army of marching cockroaches skitter across my bare feet. It feels like I'm one misstep or miscalculation away from falling on my face and proving the truth of all my self-doubt. I don't see anyone I recognize, and that's both alleviating and amplifying my anxiety. Even the fireman with water sluicing down his waist and dripping from his scruffy jaw to his carved bare chest, isn't distracting me. I watch his muscles clench while he climbs back onto the dunking platform. I should be drooling, but I'm only I'm slightly more than mildly intrigued. I know from experience that firemen might be hot, but they come with all kinds of baggage. I shake my head to dislodge the rising tide of impatience and gather my thoughts.

On the one hand, I don't need to be hyper-focused on finding exactly the right words if someone walks up to me. On the other hand, it makes the crowd seem a little ominous, like a living breathing suffocating thing tightening a noose around my neck I can't control. I feel so exposed.

I'm anonymous right now, but that won't last for long. I know it's not going to stay that way. It's only a matter of time before a student, or another teacher, forces me into awkward social interaction. I hate feeling like an off-kilter Gumby, or like a caricature of Lurch from the Addams Family, and I never know what to say and always end up unintentionally offending someone because I miss all the social cues. I'm much more comfortable in my bubble. I'm brave and relaxed when I'm swapping stories and advice and gossip with my friends.

The aroma wafting from the kettle corn booth beside me is sickly sweet, like a summer day that smells of freshly mown hay and honeycomb. I close my eyes and inhale, letting the familiar scent wash over me like a balm. The air is filled with the squeak of stroller wheels across pitted ground and uneven tussocks of grass, the plaintive wails of children, and the oohs and ahs of everyone aiming their phones at the dunking booth. Like we have a Baywatch lifeguard rising from the water instead of a bare-chested fireman. It's loud, unpredictable, chaotic, and overwhelming.

I'm exactly where she said to meet her. I've been standing here in the sweltering heat of Indian summer for forty minutes, ignoring the trickle of sweat underneath my ponytail. So far my best friend is a no-show. And she's not answering my texts.

Emma owes me an explanation for ditching me. I'm fiercely competitive, and even though this isn't a soccer field, I'm not going to forfeit my chance to win a ribbon. She knows this about me, and that's how she was able to convince me to leave my comfort zone and do this stupid race with her. After all the effort she expended persuading me to be her partner I can't believe she ditched me. I hope she's not in some kind of trouble and can't communicate. I'm angry because I hate being crippled by indecision, but I'm worried too. Which is making my skin crawl even more. It feels like a landmine I can't navigate without losing a vital organ.

I hear Taren's laugh before I see her. It's so unabashedly happy it makes my stomach cramp. There's a thread of joy running through it I've never heard. Which tells me she's with Zane. I want to rejoice with her. I really really do. I love my best friends.

But I can't swallow the hard little kernel of envy lodged in my chest like a hand grenade.

I'm trying to choke down my resentment and it feels like someone is holding the end of a lit blunt against my skin. I know I shouldn't be jealous. Taren took a chance I'm too scared to take. My fear of being rejected as not enough is like a crushing weight on the inside. I know I have even my best friends fooled. They think I'm quietly confident, instead of seeing the shivering bundle of nerves beneath my mask. I'm wired differently, and I don't know if I'll ever find someone who appreciates and loves me for it, without trying to change me or gaslight me.

I hate that Taren's unfettered happiness makes me wistful. Before the world changed, I thought my life was full and I had everything I wanted. I felt professionally fulfilled. I knew I was making a difference in the lives of the kids in our community. But lately I want someone besides my goofy dog sprawled across my bed. Even though physical touch can be difficult to handle, sometimes I just want someone to give me a bone-crushing hug at the end of a shitty day. To take my coat and push me onto the couch and force a cup of steaming Earl Grey into my hands.

I stroll up to them with studied nonchalance. They're already standing in line waiting for their burlap sack. There's a tall guy with broad shoulders and a swimmer's physique standing beside Zane. Broad shoulders, so broad I doubt my reach would meet in the middle of his back. A narrow waist, the muscled, round curve of a gluteus maximus that would make the angels weep, and thighs I can tell are as solid as the main beam of the sailboats I used to spend my summers on. The brim of his baseball cap is resting against the back of his neck, so of course that's the first thing I notice, and from the side, I can see it's hiding a man bun of honey and caramel. There are curls of black snaking like tendrils up his nape and peeking beneath the cuffs of his shirt sleeves, trailing across his biceps, and I'm sure he's hiding a tattooed canvas underneath his plain white tee. Just imagining him in a complete ensemble that includes gray sweatpants makes me want to dive into my bedside drawer full of joy tonight for relief.

Ok, enough distraction. Time to get their attention and figure out what the hell is going on. "Have any of you heard from Emma? She was supposed to be my partner."

They all turn in unison to look at me.

"Did she bail on you?" Asks Taren.

"It looks like it. And I know we would have crushed this," I observe, unable to mask the thread of irritation lacing my words.

"Yes! You are both just feral enough to obliterate the competition," laughs Taren.

"I can be your partner," a rich tenor interjects. His voice is the low rumble of thunder before heat lightning slashes across the summer sky.

It's the guy in the baseball cap. When I see his whole face I recognize him. It's the douchebag developer guy I caught Zane having lunch with. I knew there was a reason he seemed familiar. Why is he offering to be my partner? He has that delicious hint of pirate *I'll make you walk a plank alright,* and he doesn't already have a partner? Does he really want to participate or is he making a move? Is he flirting or just being nice? I thought he was Taren's enemy, and I can't believe she already buried the hatchet. Maybe he threatened her with the plank, and she feared for her life. I think Zane would've walked the plank in her stead though, or punched the guy's lights out instead of thumping him between the shoulder blades like they're the best of bros. So maybe it was just a douchebag façade, and his replenishment of the town coffers wasn't motivated by arrogance and smarminess.

He's drifted close enough that I can smell hints of bergamot, clove, and rum. Is this what it feels like to ignore the health advisory and gaze directly into the sun in the middle of an eclipse? I think my retinas are permanently scorched, and his scent makes me want to lick the sharp blade of his jaw.

"Why would you want to be my partner? You don't even know me. Don't you think it's a little soon to be getting in the sack with someone?" Crap. Am I flirting? I never flirt. I'm always too anxious to put myself out there like that. Even to myself, it sounds like I'm flirting. I shouldn't be flirting - especially when I can't tell whether he's flirting back or just being nice. Usually my attempts at flirting are either an aggressive weird version of Gru from *Despicable Me* or a cute bumbling version of Meg Ryan from a nineties rom com. And this guy is probably still a douchebag when it applies to women. Even if he's a hot douchebag. So I shouldn't even contemplate flirting with him.

Sex is usually something perfunctory for me, a necessity like food and water and air. Flirting is an unnecessary preliminary. Why spend time on the appetizer when I can shove it aside and devour the main course? Usually we don't even make it to the bed because I just need to scratch an itch, not mess up the sanctity and solace of my eight hundred thread count sanctuary or bond over an awkward breakfast of sausage gravy and biscuits.

"Is it though?" His eyes are suddenly alight with interest. I can see a glimmer of gold in the muddy brown depths. Those flecks of gold are like pyrite winking through the ripples in a creek. I'll never forget the first time one of my cousins showed me a piece she brought home from one of her Girl Scout camping trips and solemnly asked me if we should hitchhike a ride to go back and pan for more.

"Is it what?" I'm flustered because I got lost in one of my spirals trying to discern and describe the color of his eyes and have no idea what he's referring to. It's why I like numbers and scientific theory and working a problem I know has a solution that's perfectly formulated and expected. I don't have to keep track of nuanced social clues and conversations that tie me up in knots because there are so many distractions. Facts don't have surprises or meandering. They can't pull me in a thousand different directions or demand interactions beyond my control.

"Is it too soon," he clarifies. "I don't think so. Not if you want to win," he makes it sound like he's just talking about the race. The knowing glint in his gaze says otherwise. I think it's safe to conclude that he is being more than nice. That I was being paranoid again and he is actually flirting with me. "And there's no way we won't win. At least we'll beat down these two lovebirds," he cocks a thumb toward Taren and Zane, who are locked in one of their moony-eyed silent exchanges. Completely oblivious to the world. Like they always are nowadays. How they fell into this so fast after not seeing each other for seventeen years is a mystery. It's like no time passed at all.

I snort. "You're probably right. They're going to pass out from the ecstasy of having their bare legs nestled together and completely lose track of the mission," I objectively recognize that getting in the sack with this guy, proverbial or sexual, would not be a hardship.

Taren pokes me in the arm, finally rousing herself from her sexy times trance. "You won't beat us. We've been practicing."

"Please. You won't beat us," Blake interjects. "Fierce Girl and I will decimate you because of the height difference alone. You're going to pull each other down because there's like a twelve-inch span between you. You're going to trip over each other because you're so mismatched," he twists around to smirk at Zane. "Taren is going to be taking four steps for every single one of yours."

I can't tell whether I'm more amused or annoyed that he feels comfortable enough to give me a nickname on such slim acquaintance. I can tell he's the kind of guy who doles out nicknames like he's handing out candy to trick or treaters. I know we haven't done introductions, but he and Zane are obviously bros and I know my name's had to have come up in casual conversation.

As if on cue, Zane snaps out of his trance-like state. "Oh yeah. Blake, this is Sarah. Sarah, this is Blake."

Blake holds his hand out to me. I wrap my own around it because I think we're going to shake. But we don't. He's just staring down at me. Not very far. Because my eyes are even with his chin. But still not moving. "So, can I still call you Fierce Girl?"

Okay. Maybe the annoyance trumps the amusement. It annoys me that even now we've been introduced he thinks he still has the right to give me a nickname. "Do I have a choice? From everything I've heard about you, I doubt it. If you accept the fact that later on I can give you any nickname I want, I guess I'm okay with it."

"Well we're friends of our friends. Isn't it inevitable that we'll get to know each other better?" His answer is smooth. Too smooth. Like he's had a lot of practice disguising what he wants. Making it palatable even when the person on the receiving end isn't interested.

"You don't fool me. You weren't referring to the platonic form of knowing." I have zero reservations about calling him out.

"You're jumping to a lot of conclusions," he observes.

I shrug. "If the shoe fits...." I purposefully let my words trail off so he can fill in the blanks himself.

"I'll convince you I'm not a complete douchebag," he unceremoniously grabs my hand in his and leads me to the starting line. I yank away from him while simultaneously trying to calm my somersaulting sex drive. His palm is rough against my own, his grasp sure and confident. He's giving me stern brunch daddy vibes and my vajayjay is up on that vault right now with Simone Biles, strutting for all she's worth. And how does he know I think he's a douchebag? He must get that reaction a lot. Obviously he's not as smooth as he thinks he is.

He steps in and holds the bag open for me. I'm glad I wore jeans, because his basketball shorts, which are almost as drool worthy as gray sweatpants, are rolled up at the waist so almost everything below his muscled thighs is bare. Which means our skin would be touching if I'd worn shorts. I think I'm glad I wore jeans.

I once again tell my rogue lady parts to simmer down and put on my game face. It's been a while and I have to wrestle them into submission. "Let's do this."

"I don't think I've ever met anyone as competitive as I am. Until now," he gives me a huge approving grin. Okay. So he gets a point in his favor that my determination to win at all costs (even across a Monopoly board) doesn't intimidate him.

When the referee blows the whistle, we're off like a shot. We're both tall and lanky, so it's easy to match our strides. Just as predicted, we leave Taren and Zane in the dust and are soon leading the pack. The high school Phys Ed teacher and her partner gain on us when we're only a couple of lengths from the finish line. I take a bigger step and miscalculate. And down we go. As we're falling I see the eight-year-old Donaldson twins, who will soon reign terror over the entire fourth grade class, sneak past the adults and cross the finish line first.

Blake twists his body to catch the brunt of the impact. Which leaves me glued to him. My hand is resting just beneath the top of his shorts, touching the middle of a coarse trail of hair that my fingers are itching to stroke. He lost his hat, and his hair is escaping from its bun, a shaggy dark honey, caramel mess of waves around his face. With his shot of whiskey eyes, and the pale gleam of stubble on his cheeks, he's like my fantasy Thor come to life. I jerk up, but we're still tangled in the bag together.

His eyes drop to my lips before he closes them and takes a deep breath. "Let me untangle us."

Why the hell am I matching my breathing to his like we're synchronized swimmers or Lamaze partners? Why am I having trouble tearing my eyes away from him? I stare at his chin like it's the most fascinating one I've ever seen.

It kind of is, because it's carved in half, with a cleft like the one on the dad from *The Incredibles*. I'm irrationally tempted to stick my tongue there.

"Yeah," I mutter. My face is burning with the embarrassment of ten million suns. I don't need a mirror to see that even the tips of my ears are red.

Oblivious of my wayward thoughts, he deftly tosses the bag aside and lifts us to our feet. Because I'm tall, I'm not used to men moving me around so easily. I'm unbalanced for a second and involuntarily sway towards him. He catches me by the elbows. "Are you okay?" He asks.

There's no way I can get words past the lump of mortification in my throat. "Yeah," I mutter again.

He lets go. "So where do we go from here, Sarah?"

We don't go anywhere. My ovaries are acting like they just met Love Potion Number Nine. That's not a complication I need right now. I need sex that will not ruin me for all time.

"We don't go anywhere, Blake. Besides back to the sidelines with Taren and Zane."

"I don't even get a dance tonight?"

"Nope. I have lesson plans to prepare for the start of school next week," I don't feel like clarifying that this is how I prefer to spend every evening.

"What do you teach?" he sounds genuinely curious.

"I'm one of the high school science teachers. And the girls' soccer team coach."

"You sound like a workaholic, Sarah," he observes and lifts a brow like he's getting ready to proposition me. "Life shouldn't be all work and no play."

"I'm not all work and no play. I just don't want to play with you," I smugly retort.

He throws a hand to his heart, like I just shattered it, and stumbles backward.

The histrionics are ridiculous, but I still chuckle. "I'll see you around, Blake."

I need to get a grip before I agree to brave a public event that will have people packed in like sardines. For the sake of the women in this town, I hope he and Zane did not take the same salsa dancing lessons. Zane demonstrated his skills with Taren when they started dating again, and the entire restaurant was swooning. Margarita Mondays haven't been the same since.

Chapter 2

Blake

I WAS THE KID who grew up in and out of the system. The one who found gifted mittens from sympathetic teachers surreptitiously tucked into his desk after recess. The one who was grateful for the school's free breakfast and lunch program because he never knew where his next meal was coming from or if it would be anything more than a peanut butter sandwich. The one who claimed the ill-fitting winter coats from the Lost and Found. The one who fought tooth and nail to earn scholarships that would pay for college when he aged out of foster care because he knew that's the only way he would have a decent future.

After my dad died, my mom used drugs to treat her depression. Social Services pulled me out of the house more times than I can count because of her benders. She'd disappear for days looking for her next high, and when she got hooked on opioids she just stopped reporting to the social worker and dropped off the radar completely. That's when I guess she officially abandoned my little sister and me. When she finally forgot she was a mother. Her absence and being constantly shuffled around from the age of ten, resulted in emotional numbness and a deep-seated aversion to forming connections with others. It's something I'm finally coming to terms with and trying to fix after years of therapy. Now I understand why I've always found it difficult to form lasting friendships and why my bedroom has always had a revolving door. I was cocooning myself from ever having to deal with that hurt again. I wanted to be the one who left – not the one who was left.

I know now that I need to let people in, and I'm trying. I'll never be able to heal the neglected child I was, but I can build a different future.

It's the main reason I moved here and why I'm suddenly craving the close-knit community of Willow Creek. It's the antithesis of everything I was exposed to growing up. It's the antithesis of all the shallow goals I thought I needed to chase and all the insecurities I thought I needed to wrangle into submission. It's what I've managed to avoid and the thing I've always been afraid to say I wanted. It's what I think I need to finally make the desperation that claws at my soul disappear forever. It's a sense of belonging and this conviction of rightness and this affirmation of yes, you have found your place and yes, this is your tribe. It's a place that makes me feel like Luke Skywalker instead of Darth Vader, like Bruce Banner instead of The Incredible Hulk. I finally have the chance to choose my own family and I'm taking it.

If Willow Creek is my place, and Zane, Dex and Ian are my tribe, then Sarah Fraser may be my person. She's like one of those stars you can barely see with the telescope, a hazy nimbus of light you think is a galaxy. Until you adjust the focus and realize it's a supernova. She's luminous.

She's even more tightly coiled than I was before I let Willow Creek seep into my pores. And from what I understand, she's been here at least five years. I bet when she does let go it's like a Cat 8 hurricane barreling down everything in its path. Something so powerful it could level an entire city. Nothing but torrential rain and howling winds that leaves destruction in its wake. I could sense the waves of unease rolling off her and her acknowledgment of the latent attraction looming between us. She's the walking pop-up ad for "still waters run deep."

I've heard a lot about her because Zane and I are so close now. But we've never been face to face until today. I always thought of her as Fierce Girl in my head, and definitely went down a Google rabbit hole researching her soccer career. That probably makes me a creeper, something I've never been accused of because I was never intrigued enough. But the little snippets of her story Zane let slip have intrigued me from the beginning.

Now that I've met her, she totally lives up to her nickname and I think the universe was sending me a hidden message. Now that I've met her, I'm even more convinced I'm exactly where I was meant to be. Do I believe that each of us has this person we were meant to find? I don't know. Maybe. I wouldn't have believed in that shit before I came to Willow Creek. But after seeing Taren and Zane together it seems like a definite possibility. Do I believe in love at first sight? Definitely not. But there's an invisible thread between us I can't explain. She tugs at something deep inside me that I've ignored and kept buried for a long time.

I was stuck in a sack with her for less than ten minutes and I can't get her out of my mind. Yes, I'm attracted to her. But this pull is way more than that and I'd be a fool not to pursue it. I swear I thought we were having a moment at the end of the race when every inch of her was plastered against me. It turned me on more than any of the former beauty queens stripping down in my apartment. Her dismissal was so brusque, and her departure was so abrupt, I must have been hallucinating. I'm hoping that she was brusque because she felt the pull between us too and she was doing her best to ignore it because it was unexpected.

Zane invited me over for beer and burgers before the concert in the park tonight, and I plan on picking his brain. We're sitting in his gargantuan backyard, relaxing on a couple of loungers with a perimeter of citronella torches surrounding us. The farmhouse looms in the background, like a sprawling welcome mat straight out of *The Waltons*. Ian is at the firehouse tonight, probably on kitchen duty there, but Dex is manning the grill in his stead. The charred smell of a charcoal fired quarter pounder has my mouth watering. I'm drinking one of the hard ciders Zane and Taren distilled this year, and the taste is a cross between apple pie and tart cherries. I decide it's the perfect time to find out exactly how to get under Sarah's skin. I don't want him to immediately guess I'm interested, so I go for subtlety. "So what's the deal with Taren's friend Sarah? She seemed a little prickly?"

Zane laughs. "Prickly? Like a hedgehog? Or like a wasp?" His question seems innocuous, but I know it's not. He's fishing for information, channeling an attention to detail and a focus like Sherlock Holmes. He's scary sometimes, like a diviner in front of a mirror. It's why I always secretly dreaded placing a bid on any property I knew he was interested in – he has a bloodhound way of sensing the undercurrents of any situation.

I grin sheepishly. "Hedgehogs are cute and cuddly. She's very self-contained and gives off the vibe of *"touch me and I'll slice your fingers off."* I'm definitely leaning towards the wasp."

He cocks an inquisitive brow in my direction. "So you're interested? Even if you're in imminent danger of swelling in the infected area?" He guffaws at his own innuendo. When he finally stops laughing at his own joke, he badgers me further. "I thought you might be after all those questions, even if you were trying to disguise it behind your casual facade. And you were peppering me with those before you ever actually met her."

I roll my eyes. Ok. So obviously I wasn't subtle enough. But if not so subtly digging is what will get me answers, then so be it. "What if I am? And dude, yes, before you ask, she already makes me swell inconveniently."

Zane and his friend Dex burst into raucous laughter and exchange what can only be described as a weighted glance. "Can't say I'm surprised," surmises Zane. "It definitely looked like the two of you became cozy while you were laying in the grass."

"It took us a while to get our bearings," I clarify, smirking.

"Uh-huh. I'll bet it did. Your ball bearings," mutters Dex under his breath loud enough for us to hear. And then he snorts. And so does Zane. They're like a couple of thirteen-year-olds snickering in the locker room over a copy of the *Sports Illustrated Swimsuit Edition*.

"I can't believe you let a pair of eight-year-olds pulverize you. You guys were way ahead of the pack with the Phys Ed teachers hot on your heels, and then Bam! Down you went," jibes Zane when they're done laughing at my predicament.

"The determination of those kids was downright terrifying. I can easily believe they have a future ahead of them that consists of world domination. Sarah and I were victims of our own clumsiness and I think we would've won if we'd had the opportunity to practice together before the main event," I'm very confident of this. Her long legs were perfectly suited to my stride. And I know I just met her, but I can't stop imagining them wrapped around my waist in the middle of a wall banger.

"Oh! So you want a rematch," chortles Zane. I reel my thoughts back into the present. These assholes will rib me even more if they know how much she's consuming my thoughts. Even though I know beyond the shadow of a doubt that Zane is just as attuned to Taren, and I suspect Dex is downright miserable anytime he's in the vicinity of Marianela.

The fact that Zane thinks he's hilarious is beyond irritating. "I didn't say that."

"Well it sounds like you didn't quite get your fill of the lovely, inscrutable Ms. Fraser. Would you like my help remedying that situation? Do you want me to get you insider information? I can gather important intel since she's one of Taren's best friends," he leans forward excitedly, his elbows on his knees.

"You look kind of rabid right now. I'm not sure if that's a wise decision on my part – seeking your help. You're like a dog chasing a whole family of rabbits that disappeared down a hole you can't fit your snout into," I rake my hands through my hair, and lean back, clasping my arms behind my head. I stare up at the cloudy sky like I'm mesmerized. I don't need his meddling to tip her off. "Taren will see right through your ploy and then Sarah will know I've been asking about her. I don't want to give myself away so easily. I need this to happen organically," I think he's one of those guys so happy in love he wants everyone else to be too. I wonder why he's not putting this much effort into Dex as well. Then again, I don't know what's happening behind the scenes. He did tell me about the tense situation that happened at the Mexican restaurant last month.

This place has turned him into a completely different person. One I never would've suspected of existing behind the Ray bans and Armani suit that was always outbidding me for prime real estate. He was ruthless. Now he's in battered jeans and a t-shirt every time I see him. Or worn flannel since the nights are turning colder. He looks like a farmer or a lumberjack. He even has a beard now and doesn't seem ruthless at all. It's like he's lost his edge and he doesn't regret leaving it behind. I wonder if I can shed my second skin and if I'll regret leaving it behind.

"Well it may interest you to know that the high school is now short one varsity soccer coach," he interrupts my bout of introspection.

"Why would that interest me? I've never coached in my life," I played high school and college soccer, but never pursued it as a career. I was able to admit to myself that I didn't have the skills to play at that level. Now I'm wondering if this is somehow related to her since she let me know she's the girls' soccer coach.

He shrugs. "The school board is desperate. It's unpaid, and they can't find anyone. But you don't need the money. Taren's brother, Trevor was the coach the last four seasons. But he just moved to Philadelphia," he explains.

"Why is this something I should look into?" I'm baffled by his insistence, unless this is the Jedi mind trick I've been searching for.

"Because Sarah Fraser is the varsity coach of the girls' team. Boom! Forced proximity." He claps his hands together so loudly; I almost spill my beer.

"Yeah, I knew she was the coach. But I don't think that's the secret formula for romance, "I skeptically reply.

Dex doesn't even bother controlling his laughter as he gives Zane a disbelieving look. "Dude, that book club is warping your masculinity. Forced proximity doesn't always lead to romance."

Zane shakes his head in disagreement. "Laugh all you want. Because I am. I'm laughing all the way to the bedroom. And the shower. And wherever I feel like laughing. I guarantee I'm laughing way more often than either of you," he smugly observes. "It's a trope for a reason. That shit really does happen in real life," he defensively concludes. So defensively I honestly believe he'd willingly die on his own samurai sword on the top of that mountain.

I have a feeling they'll be arguing like two old codgers chewing hayseed on the bench outside the general store if I don't intervene. Even though I suspect he's full of himself, maybe I'm desperate enough to try whatever he suggests. Even though I'm wondering how reading romance teaches you to ensnare women. "Say I think your idea has merit. How do I go about landing this awesome unpaid gig?" There's more than a hint of sarcasm, which I know he'll ignore. He's so happy now he's shitting nothing but sunshine.

He waves a hand. "I've got your back," so he completely missed my sarcasm. Or just chose to ignore it. "The principal was my co-captain and middle linebacker in high school."

Of course he was. These small towns are like a perilous sticky web full of green bottleflies. I guess that means I'm the granddaddy longlegs – kind of watching from the outskirts. Even though I feel like an outsider with my nose pressed against the glass, I appreciate any assistance he can give me. I've never been more intrigued by a woman. I'm even willing to test his theory about forced proximity fanning the flames higher. "That'd be awesome, man. I'd love to kick the ball around the field again," I reply. Kicking the ball around would be a great outlet for all the restless energy swirling around in my chest. And I always wanted to join the Big Brother program in the city but could never seem to fit it into my schedule. This may be my only chance to mentor kids who might be like the one I once was.

"Well, you'll get your chance. Especially since you're not asking for a salary. They're pretty desperate and your reputation as a savior for filling the town coffers precedes you. They'll bend over backwards to be accommodating," he assures me.

"Do you think my reputation has made an impression on Ms. Fraser?" I doubt it, but I could be wrong.

"Not a chance. You have your work cut out for you, dude," observes Dex, shaking his head in sympathy.

"Unfortunately, man, I have to side with Dex on this one," Zane shakes his head and claps me on the shoulder.

"I'll weaken her defenses eventually. There's nothing like good old-fashioned competition to let go of your inhibitions."

"This is going to be so much fun to watch," Zane comments with a wink in Dex's direction.

"Watch and learn, my friends," they'll be eating their words. And if I'm going to chip away at her defenses I need a place to stay that's an improvement over my current lodgings. "Have either of you heard of anything for rent? It'll be at least nine months until the farmhouse is renovated, and all the barns and outbuildings are up. Meanwhile I need someplace to lay my head that isn't covered in doilies and embroidered pillows," while I appreciate the willingness of Mrs. Snead to permit me to stay as a long-term guest at her bed and breakfast, I feel like I'm tiptoeing through a museum. Or a kitschy flea market stall. There are way too many frilly, dainty things in pastel colors that ooze genteel Victorian shabby chic.

She also has three ginormous Persian cats that watch me with beady eyes. It reminds me too much of Dolores Umbrage's office. My penthouse in Fairfax is furnished solely in shades of gray because I find them calming, and I don't have to share my meals with only cats for company. I think there's a reason Sweet Pea's Bed and Breakfast was the only lodging with available rooms.

Dex gives me a considering look, like he's deciding whether to tell me something. "I think I know of a place," he cryptically replies.

"Dude, that's great! I'm sick of living out of a suitcase. And I might be tempted to flush every single doily I see down the toilet if I don't escape soon. Where is it?"

"It's one of the cabins on the lake. It's a little rustic, but it has everything you'll need, plus a whole house generator as a power backup. It's a far cry from the penthouse Zane's told me you own, but it will save you from the possessed stares of Winken, Blinken and Nod."

"So everyone knows about the Persians? And the Umbrage vibes?" I feel slighted they didn't bother to warn me.

"We had a bet going on how long you could tolerate it," Zane confesses with a grin. "I won because Dex said you'd only last a week. You lasted almost a month, and we're both very impressed by your fortitude. If you can be that patient in an environment like that, wooing Sarah Fraser should be a piece of cake."

"I don't think she's going to be a piece of cake. I think she's going to be the furthest thing from it. I think getting her to go on a date will be almost impossible. But I love a challenge," I want to rub my hands together like the Pied Piper or something. "I don't need fancy. I just need somewhere private to relax and unwind. Who do I need to speak to?"

"Actually, it's mine," Dex surprises me. "It's one of my rental properties. I had a tenant there for three years and he just moved out earlier this month. I've had it cleaned and was planning on doing some remodeling before I leased it out again, but if you want it, it's yours."

"I definitely want it. Airdrop me a copy of the lease and I'll have a signed copy in your hands tomorrow."

"You may not want it when you hear the rest," he cautions me.

"I doubt that – it sounds perfect." And it does. Because honestly anything is better than having nightmares about the doilies.

"Then again, it melds quite nicely with your other plans. Your closest neighbor is Ms. Fraser," he watches me speculatively, tapping his finger against his chin.

"So I'll be seeing a lot of her?" Suddenly I'm anticipating things like watching her mow her yard in a bikini.

"Not necessarily," Zane chortles. "Each cabin sits on just under five acres and both lots are heavily wooded. But you know. Forced proximity," he waggles his eyebrows like a ten-year-old.

I'm disappointed, but I don't let it show. It's still close enough that I can sneak over to borrow a cup of sugar. Or bring her a mug of morning coffee. Or offer to clean the leaves from her gutters and shovel her driveway when it snows. Acts of service seem like a surefire way to earn my way into her good graces.

Chapter 3

Sarah

I ALWAYS LOOK FORWARD to the first day of school. It's one of my favorite days of the year because it's filled with hope and possibility. Starting the day after Labor Day, the officially unofficial end to the lazy days of summer, is the perfect segue into fall and chilly home football games and bonfires. Don't get me wrong. I love cookouts and margaritas and mojitos and all the summer cocktails on the water with my besties. But I love fall more. The crisp air always smells like burnt cinnamon to me and I count down the days until I can break out my Frye boots and my leggings.

We've been in lockdown for almost two years, and I should be anticipating the promise of tomorrow more than I ever have. I'm anticipating it, but not in a good way. I have this knot in my stomach that I can't dispel. Nothing has helped. Not even listening to "Zombie" by *The Cranberries* or "Ice Cream" by *Sarah MacLachlan* or "I'm Sensitive" by *Jewel*. Those songs are my automatic get in the zone anthems. I can always lose myself in the lyrics and sway around my living room. My cousins and I used to dance around to my aunt's 90s cd collection and listening to that music always sends me to my happy place. When the inevitable rift happened between my mom and her sister, I missed those days with a pang I still haven't recovered from.

I have this sinking feeling something is going to happen that I won't be able to control. That something about this year is going to be momentous and raw. I know I'm not ready for whatever is coming. I need to be distracted from worrying about it and reassured that everything will be okay. The only people who can give me that are Taren and Emma. I invited them over for dinner and a movie.

I have Guardians of the Galaxy queued up for tonight. Groot always makes me feel better. He's my favorite because everyone thinks he's cute and harmless when he's exactly the opposite. He doesn't say much, but he's not afraid to let you know how he feels and doesn't care who he offends. When I was growing up, everyone saw me as cute and harmless. The sweet quiet little blonde girl who tried to fit herself into a box and let out all her aggression run free on the soccer field. That's the only place I wore my ferocious heart on my sleeve.

Even though I know every single word by heart, there's something about watching that movie unfold, and seeing the dynamic level of snark as Gamora hands Star Lord his ass on a platter, that makes me happy. Taren and Emma will roll their eyes, but they love it too. Especially the soundtrack. The Redbone song is on our karaoke list for the next open mic night at Guy's. This is how I know I've found my tribe. They don't think twice about my quirkiness because they openly admit to their own weirdness. The last time we drank together we had a very enlightening conversation about toe hair on men, and whether it was attractive or disgusting. Which of course led to an even weirder conversation about the mechanics of banging a hobbit versus the mechanics of banging an elf or a dwarf. We all concluded that a dwarf with the voice of Richard Armitage would be worth any contortionism necessary. It's crossed my mind that the guy I can't stop thinking about has the same last name and an equally mesmerizing voice.

I'm making chicken fettucine because it's easy and it's my favorite. Taren volunteered to bring the salad, and of course Emma is bringing dessert. She spends every spare minute she has coming up with new recipes, and her new Spiced Apple Cider and Apple Brown Betty cupcakes are debuting this week. She said she was inspired by the success of Taren's business. She and Zane are making their mark on the cider industry and just released new batches. They even sponsored the town's Apple Festival. Where I ended up tangled in a sack with Blake.

I'm setting the table out on the deck when they show up. I started a fire in the pit, and just opened a bottle of Sauvignon Blanc.

We're sitting in the Adirondack chairs, on our second bottle of Sauvignon Blanc, when Taren finally asks the question I know has been on the tip of her tongue all night.

"So, Sarah. What did you think of Blake?" She's looking at me expectantly.

"He seems nice," I don't want to talk about the way he made me want more than a perfunctory, utilitarian fuck.

"Nice," I can feel her eyes piercing my soul, determined to scour out the truth. "Huh. I thought I'd get more than a "nice" from you after your tumble into the grass. You were flushed after the fall, and there was an undercurrent to your conversation with him."

I'm flushing now. I feel the heat creeping into my cheeks because she's backed me into a corner. I thought she was too wrapped up in Zane to notice the undercurrents.

"Leave her alone, Taren. She obviously doesn't want to talk about it," Emma comes to my rescue. "Especially since the whole town knows he's the new boys' soccer coach," she winks and gives me a conspiratorial grin I choose to ignore.

That had not been welcome news. I heard the rumors during my breakfast at Cupcake on Main this morning. And then Principal Greene called earlier this evening and confirmed it. He sounded way too ecstatic about finding a soccer coach for a mediocre team. He's part of the old boys' club, though, so I shouldn't be surprised by his enthusiasm. "It's not that I don't want to talk about it. Not necessarily," I swallow the last of my wine, letting the grapefruit and peach undertones rest at the back of my throat while I formulate my answer. After endless seconds of silent expectation, I set my glass on the side table. I twist my fingers in my lap and brace myself for what I'm about to say. "It's just that I'm not sure how he made me feel. I'm used to treating sex like a necessary evil. I indulge in it with the sole aim of self-satisfaction," I stare at the flames beneath the grate and try to figure out how to put what I felt into words. "He made me wonder if maybe utilitarian sex isn't enough."

Taren's eyes go wide at my confession. "So you two were flirting," she concludes. "And that flirting made you want more. We've never seen you go on more than one date with someone, but we know you like one-night-stands because you've shared the details with us before. Why do you think this guy has the potential to make you want more?"

"At first I couldn't tell if he was just being nice," Taren gives me a disbelieving look. "Then it became obvious he was flirting with me like I was the peanut butter to his banana," Taren and Emma both snort at this comparison.

"I bet he wishes you were the peanut butter plastered on his banana," Emma mumbles so low I can barely hear it. Of course we all erupt into laughter.

Once we're not about to fall out of our chairs like bone-less starfish, I give her a mock glare. "You're one to talk.

You're always talking about the bananas the firemen carry in their pockets," I shoot back. She just winks at my salvo. "Anyway, long story short. I couldn't stop myself from flirting back. I don't know why. I've never been someone that flirts. I mean what's the point? When that spark is there, both people know they want to get horizontal, or bang against a wall or another convenient surface, so why waste time flirting when they can just get down to it?" I shrug.

Emma seems completely mesmerized by my matter-of-fact explanation of why flirting is a wasted endeavor. "Flirting can enhance the anticipation," she observes. "But I can see the appeal in your approach too. It's exactly how I always imagined men approached sex, like an animal instinct," she taps her thumb and forefinger against her chin, like she's going to squirrel that conclusion away and eventually ponder it in greater detail. "Please teach me your ways, Wise One. I would love to be able to relegate sex to the sidelines like it's just another bodily function. So I can just say things like, oh it must be time for a fuck. Or a fuck sounds great right about now, the perfect thing to put me to right," she raises her glass in a toast. "Woman, you are the liberated version of sexuality I strive to be."

I laugh, a little embarrassed at her admiration. I thought they knew this about me, that it wouldn't come as a surprise. "I don't think of myself as liberated. Sometimes I feel like I'm a kite that's barely tethered in the branches of a tree, the string tangled and knotted up," I squint into the distance, staring at the deep purple of the sunset sinking beyond the hills. "It always feels like I'm on the verge of either soaring or crashing to the ground. Because I never know what to expect or what the world will throw at me next," I've never revealed this much to them. It's not that I don't trust them, there are just certain defining parts of me I don't share with anyone. I'm pretty sure it's not the wine loosening my tongue and my inhibitions. Somehow that annoying pirate with his pyrite eyes is having this effect on me. I resent him for it - even as the image of me looking over my shoulder to find him prowling closer scrambles my brain.

What I don't tell them is I treat sex like a transaction because sometimes physical touch can be challenging if the environment is overstimulating or if I have too many thoughts careening around in my head. Sometimes my brain just won't shut up long enough to enjoy it. If I make the sex transactional it's a lot easier to detach myself from the nuances of the experience.

Taren looks at me thoughtfully. "Sometimes you just need the right person to be your goalie when everyone's throwing balls at you. I'm going to give you the same advice you gave me. If you're attracted to him, chase those orgasms. You deserve every single one."

"I knew that's what you were going to tell me. I'm surprised you didn't give that advice as soon as we sat down. I gave you that exact same advice about Zane. He must be teaching you to be patient."

She blushes so brightly it's blinding.

"You have kinky stories to share. We can tell," Emma flourishes her hands in Taren's direction. "They won't be shared tonight because we all have early mornings. But I'm not letting you off the hook."

Emma still hasn't told us anything about where she was the day of the festival. She apologized for leaving me in the lurch and just said she had something to take care of. Something she couldn't put off any longer. Her Le Baron wasn't parked in front of Cupcake on Main when I drove past on my way home that night. I think whatever she had to take care of was happening somewhere else and was about whatever she's running from.

They both give me hugs before they leave. Most of the time, my sensory processing disorder makes hugs challenging. There's something about certain fabrics, such as wool and certain polyesters, that physically agitates me. I loathe wearing socks. I'd love to spend my life barefoot or in sandals. My days of wearing cleats were sheer torture.

This time, I welcome the hugs. It's their way of showing me they care and understand. I think they may suspect the challenges I face, but neither of them has said anything. They just accept me for who I am and support me no matter what.

The next morning, I eye myself critically in the mirror. I defaulted to one of my favorite ensembles – a sensible cardigan set. It's a soft periwinkle cashmere with sedate pearl buttons. I think Emma would call it elevated chic instead of frumpy. At least that's what I hope she'd call it. I'm probably being too optimistic about her commentary. I paired it with a pencil skirt instead of slacks, and my reflection tells me I look more than presentable. You can't tell my palms are sweaty or I have chills running up and down my spine. I want to channel the vibe of unruffled calm. I want to channel the town librarian, Ms. Bromwell. She gives the impression that she is completely unflappable. Maybe a little part of me wants to convince the new boys' soccer coach that I'm completely impervious to his charms. Mr. Armitage's presence has been requested at the morning assembly when all new staff will be introduced to the student body and the tingles skating up and down my spine make me feel like I'm in a roller derby.

Since I'm wearing a skirt, I opt to drive my truck instead of riding my bike. All the boys immediately crowd around me when I pull into a staff parking spot. They love my vintage ride and are always pestering me about it.

"Hey Coach Fraser, when are you gonna let me drive your truck in the homecoming parade?," yells the school quarterback, as if on cue. He wore the crown last year and will most likely be wearing it again this year.

"Never, Mr. Stinson," I inform him as I shut the door. "There's no doubt in my mind that you are clueless when it comes to operating a manual transmission. You need to rectify that at some point if you ever want a sportscar that matches your ego." Daniel Stinson, the cocky senior quarterback, has been asking the same question since before he even had a permit. And I've always given the same answer. There's no way I would let a cocky teenage boy drive my truck. Especially one I know for a fact is a daredevil. I have it on good authority that he's one of the sole reasons the sheriff's deputies stake out the straight stretch of road between State Route 128 and Greenback Road. He likes to think of himself as the modern-day version of a hero from *American Graffiti*. He's a kid whose parents have given him everything he ever wanted, and he can do no wrong in their eyes. When he eventually grows up and realizes the world outside of the Willow Creek microcosm isn't full of people pleasers and adoring fans, he'll have a rude awakening.

Gramps and I spent two years of afterschool evenings lovingly restoring my powder blue 1962 International C100. It was a way for us to claim valuable time together, and having my hands occupied with tools meant my mind was occupied too. It's my one memory of a time I didn't feel pressured or stressed to be someone other than myself. Being in his garage and listening to his collection of Motown while we tinkered was a blessed escape from the stifling expectations at home. It's the one time in my life I felt I was enough just as I was. Because of those precious memories, I'm never letting anyone else drive it. Especially a teen daredevil. I drove it all the way across the country when I settled here and it's the one piece of home I'll never let go. I've let everything else sift through my fingers like grains of sand, but never this.

When I sling my messenger bag over my shoulder and head towards the entrance, I notice the newest staff addition. He's leaning against a motorcycle. He has his tousled waves scraped back in a manbun, and his arms are crossed over his chest, the tendrils of his tattoos peeking from beneath his sleeves. He's watching me with this irrepressible smirk – like I've somehow surprised him. He unfolds his long lean length away from his bike and strides toward me. I expect the ground to quake the way his stealthy approach makes me quake inside. I'm mesmerized despite myself, and very, very curious about his mode of transportation. I have a bone-deep fear of motorcycles, but I can't help admitting that he's straight from the pages of an MC romance. He has just the right hint of bad boy and vigilante Robin Hood.

"So, Fierce Girl. I should've known your vehicle would be as unique as you," his whiskey dark eyes are skating over me like I'm on the dessert menu.

We fall into step beside each other. "I'm assuming you meant that as a compliment."

"It was a compliment. Not only are you a girl with a truck – you're a girl with a classic truck. A classic truck with a manual transmission. Do you have any idea how sexy that is to a gearhead like me?," he asks with a hint of awe and disbelief.

"Being sexy was never my intention," I scoff. I'll never give him the satisfaction of knowing that today's ensemble was carefully selected to throw him off his game. To make me seem completely untouchable. But of course he's a gearhead and we have that in common. "If I'd known it would send your pheromones into a frenzy, I would've borrowed Emma's Le Baron."

"That would've been a tragedy," his voice is low and smooth and loaded with innuendo. "I'd love to ruffle you up. Your hair is even in a bun. It's like the gods are trying to punish me."

"It must bear repeating that my outfit and my truck are not meant to entice the opposite sex," I sternly reiterate. His attention is making me nervous, and I have this almost overwhelming urge to bite my nails. Even though I stopped doing that at least five years ago.

"Trust me, I know. You're the only woman I've ever met who seems completely immune to me and my charms," he ruefully observes. He doesn't seem deterred by my lack of interest. He seems intrigued by it. Why do men always want what they sense is beyond their reach?

"I know better than to let my guard down for playboys – no matter how charming they're," I turn toward a door in the middle of the hallway. "This classroom is mine. I suggest you find something to occupy your time until the assembly."

He's standing so still he could be one of those statues in the garden of the White Witch from Narnia, an intense Mr. Tumnus carved from marble. Forever frozen in time, his gaze somehow both hot and desperate, like he can't help watching me. I quietly close the door on him and resolve to close it quietly on my rioting thoughts as well. I don't know why he makes my heart flutter in my chest, like the fragile wings of a songbird trapped in the claws of a Great Horned Owl, but I don't like my visceral reaction to him. Blake Armitage is trouble with a capital T.

Chapter 4

Blake

THAT PENCIL SKIRT. AND that fucking cardigan. The way everything is pasted to her lithe curves like glue, hugging the curve of her ass and accentuating the length of her legs. Sheer torture. She should look like a dowdy school-marm, or a character from *The Little House on the Prairie.* She doesn't. She looks exactly like the present I hope to find under my Christmas tree this year. I want to unwrap her. There's just enough Grinch in my heart to want to squeeze down the chimney and steal her. I want to slip every single one of those tiny little pearl buttons loose so I can ease the cashmere slowly down the rounded curves of her shoulders, like a whisper of silk, and sip at the gleam of sweat against the satin skin of her nape.

When Principal Greene introduces me, the entire audi-torium erupts into cheers and applause. The enthusiasm is unwarranted, and I'm not sure why the crowd is so enthusiastic. I make a cocky bow nonetheless, and Fierce Girl rolls her eyes. She's not impressed by my reception or my antics.

All the attention I'm receiving should be gratifying. Two of my new colleagues have discreetly pressed scraps of paper into my hands. I don't need to look to know they have phone numbers scrawled across them. But no, that wasn't gratifying enough. Instead, my eyes stray toward the aloof, icy blonde who is very studiously ignoring me. I want to rile her composure, make her simmer, and catch fire. I remember scoffing at Zane when he talked about wanting to do that to Taren, how he got such a rush from making her lose her temper. And now I understand what he was talking about. I want to provoke a reaction. Any reaction.

I stroll off the stage and casually approach her. "So Ms. Fraser. What did you think of the assembly?"

"I think you made quite the impression on the female students and staff. And some of the male ones as well," she observes with wry amusement.

I know I should be embarrassed, but I'm not. I'm used to the attention my looks garner. I never lack for attention from the opposite sex – even though I don't look like your typical clean-cut upstanding businessman. My opponents always underestimate my shrewdness. They expect a play-boy, and though I see no harm in being self-indulgent, that's far from the sum of who I am. Here in Willow Creek they still put me in a box. It's not just my bad boy reputation they find enticing – it's my money too. They think I'm the best catch here. They don't know that up until this point I refused to be caught. Until I met the woman standing in front of me right now who's laying the trap. I'd gladly step into a set of steel jaws and risk being maimed if I knew she was the one holding the key. "Not everyone is as determined to resist my charms as you."

"I think that's half my appeal to you. The fact that you can't tell if you get under my skin," she's watching me in fascination. "You're like the bird with the brightest plumage, preening its feathers and demanding all the attention."

"Do I get under your skin? Do you enjoy my preening?" I've noticed her gaze straying to my biceps, and I can't forget the hitch in her breath when she was sprawled over me beneath that burlap sack. I hope I get under her skin so much she'll never be able to scrape me away. Like a barnacle clinging precariously to the hull of a ship. I hope she's just so self-contained and capable of teaching a master class on denial, that what she's hiding is completely invisible. And I hope she's hiding a bone-crushing attraction to me. I hope that she can't stop thinking about me.

"If you do, I'll never admit it. You'll just have to wonder. I know better than to lay that power at your feet," she scoffs.

"You're cruel to leave me wondering," her response wasn't even coy. It was given without the slightest hesitation, very matter of fact. Like she couldn't care less how she affects me.

"Why am I cruel?" There's a little crease between her brows, like no one's ever accused her of cruelty. Like she can't fathom why I would. But then the corner of her mouth curls into a smile, like she's secretly pleased. Like it's a compliment she never expected but welcomes.

"Because you make me work harder than I've ever had to," I hadn't realized that was the truth until I just put it out there into the universe. She makes me work harder because I've never wanted anything or anyone as badly as I want her.

"If I'm cruel, you're spoiled. We should all have to work hard for what we want," she says over her shoulder as she turns away. Now she's not even trying to hide her smile. I catch the curve of it across her apple of her cheek as she leaves me standing there. I'm never the one left standing alone like a tongue-tied, gaping teen.

A solid hand claps me in the middle of the back. "Good luck. In the five years she's been here, I've never heard of her going on a date."

I turn around, surprised by the sentiment and the observation. I'm glad it's not just me she's immune to. Apparently she's just allergic to all potential relationships. I wonder what happened to make her so untouchable. I want to find out. The man facing me is wider than a defensive linebacker, his teeth gleaming white against his mahogany skin. He holds out a hand to shake. "Seth Murray at your service. Health Sciences teacher, Drivers Ed instructor and football coach. I'm glad we'll have another guy on staff. Sometimes it's a little like a henhouse around here. There's too little testosterone."

Sometimes too little testosterone is a good thing, but I laugh despite myself. "And I take it you and the other guys feel like the lone roosters?"

"Without a doubt. You've got your work cut out for you. And it doesn't help that the boys' and girls' soccer teams are competing against each other for a very small amount of funding and attention. Like most small towns in America, people set their clocks by the Friday night lights. My football team takes up most of the sports budget, even though we've been on a losing streak for years."

"There's a rivalry between the soccer teams?" I should've known. I'm sure it's only made worse by the fact that many professional women's leagues, no matter what the sport, are controlled by white, cishet men who have created a culture of homophobia and fetishization. Women's teams get less attention, less praise, and less respect because of this lopsided equation. Just another example of how the cultural conversation and subtext around sports and athletic abilities needs to change. I hope my presence here will move the dialogue forward instead of hindering it.

"Oh yeah. The girls' team is much better. Because Ms. Fraser brings the big guns to the fight. She was second string for the Olympics. She knows Mia Hamm. Like personally," he informs me reverently. "Can you imagine that?"

This insight doesn't surprise me. She glows too brightly for Willow Creek, and it's obvious to anyone who takes the time to pay attention that she is hiding in plain sight. Deliberately shoving her light into a forgotten, albeit pleasant, backwater.

"I like a challenge," I tell Coach Murray. This isn't a lie. I just hope this challenge doesn't leave me looking like a bloody, broken mess on the side of the road.

She has way more kids trying out for her team than I do for mine. When Murray told me about the dismal prospects and lackluster former season of the boys' team I thought he was exaggerating. Obviously, he wasn't. I don't even have enough kids for a second-string line-up. I'm looking at a small throng of fifteen guys. Can I really afford to cut any of them? Even if I keep them all, some of the positions will be on the field for the entire game. It means they might be more prone to injury because of exhaustion. I want to ensure we have a winning season, but it has all the hallmarks of a disaster waiting to happen. I'm afraid it won't help me prove myself to the woman of my dreams without unintentionally stealing her thunder. I'm convinced that nothing will accomplish my goals like coaching my team to a winning season, and somehow making it clear that both school soccer teams deserve as much attention and undying devotion as the football team. If I'm going to do that, I have to build up fragile adolescent egos and try not to infringe on the gains she's made with the girls' team. It feels like a herculean task.

Chapter 5

Sarah

I CAN'T BELIEVE HOW many girls showed up for tryouts this year. We made it to the state finals last year and lost the title by one penalty point. It was the best season ever for the team and two of my senior players got full-ride scholarships. The median gross income for a family of four in Willow Creek is around sixty-five thousand. All the manufacturing jobs disappeared a long time ago, and we're too far from the interstate to lure light industrial warehouses here. Now it's mostly a farming community, small shops and family-owned companies barely eking by, and the occasional medical professional, accountant, or teacher. That gross income's a little higher than the national average, but it still means that most of these kids won't be able to afford college unless they assume a substantial amount of student loan debt. Landing a scholarship means they won't have to bear that burden. So I have around thirty girls vying for spots on the team. That means eight girls won't have a place in first or second string, and I have to let them down easily without crushing their hopes.

I lift the whistle to my lips, ready to signal it's time to run drills. And then Blake Armitage prowls onto the field. He's dressed in gray sweatpants that disguise nothing. It's like he found some hidden memo that this look is crack to my libido. Or maybe he secretly reads romance and knows exactly how to tie women up in knots with nothing more than a strategic wardrobe choice. Even from this distance, I can see how the thin fleece is molded to him, highlighting, and caressing the flex of his thighs as he strides toward me.

I gulp because it's a distraction I don't need right now. I mentally pinch myself to tear my gaze away.

His whole team is trailing behind him. There aren't very many of them. Less than twenty. I shouldn't feel smug about my superior turnout because he has his work cut out for him and we all play for the same school. But I am smug. I can't help it. It's freaking amazing to see a boys' team get a smaller share of the spotlight for once. Armitage will be lucky if he can even manage enough players for a complete second string. I should probably pity him for the headaches he has to look forward to. Instead I rejoice in the fact that his arrogance will be taken down a notch or two.

He approaches me with an over-the-top grin. "Good afternoon, Ms. Fraser."

"Good afternoon, Coach Armitage," I emphasize. Letting him know he needs to address me like an equal in front of both teams. That I have the title of coach for a reason, that I've earned the right to claim it.

"You have quite the turnout," he gestures towards the sea of eager faces behind me.

"Well, we have a winning record. Not exactly what the boys' team is known for," I can't help smirking.

"Well I intend to change that," he states with conviction.

"You have your work cut out for you. It looks like you don't even have enough players for your second string," I innocently observe.

"No. But when we start winning we'll get more players," he asserts, like both winning and recruiting more players is a foregone conclusion. He tips his head towards me in acknowledgement and ambles back to his team. He must lose awareness of me because he's busy wielding his whistle like Captain Von Trapp. That shouldn't be another turn-on, but of course it is. I mean, there's a reason so many women want to be a problem like Maria.

We're still working on footwork when he wraps up his practice. I steadfastly ignore his departure.

Sasha is waiting at the door when I get home. I can tell she's been eager for a swim all day because she shoots between my legs and heads straight for the shoreline once I deposit my bag on the floor. I follow her out there and kick off my shoes, sinking my toes in the gritty sand. The wind is briskly teasing the treetops, and I think summer is finally coming to an end. I'm glad of today's wardrobe choice. Both for the warmth and the fact that Blake Armitage had a hard time looking away.

The lake stretches in front of me, an endlessly serene mirror that reflects the shoreline crowded with trees. The breeze brushing my hair smells slightly acrid, like a musky-sweet pile of leaves, and I know the earth has started hunkering down for winter. Soon it'll be too cold to stand here barefoot. The cold won't deter my determined Husky – she revels in that kind of weather. But I loathe it. I grew up on the rainy west coast, and it rarely got into the teens temperature wise, even in the depths of winter's grip. It does that here on a regular basis, and even when it's not that cold, the wind can be brutal enough to make it feel like I'm on an Arctic expedition. I just want it to be eternally autumn. At least I could mimic the hibernation of a grumpy bear during the pandemic.

When I finally insist Sasha leave the water she gives me one of her *"fine, Mom, you're such a party-pooper"* looks and follows me back up the pathway with her tail tucked between her legs. I need to get her out in the canoe this weekend so we can have a sunny afternoon of fishing and romping. We haven't been out in at least three weeks, and I know it'll calm us both and give her the bonding time she needs.

A truck I've never seen is parked at the end of the driveway next door. The bed is filled with boxes, and I can make see the outline of the IKEA logo on a couple of them. The only other furniture it's holding is a big leather recliner. Apparently I have a new neighbor moving in and that neighbor is a guy. Only a guy would think a recliner was more important than a bed and consider it the most essential piece of furniture. Dex told me he had a lot of updates to do before he rented out the cabin next to mine, so I'm surprised to see he decided to lease it to someone. I was looking forward to having this stretch of the beach to myself, and not having to deal with anyone intruding on my solitude. I crave my peace and quiet, so I hope they respect my privacy and keep the noise and interference to a minimum.

Chapter 6

Blake

EVEN VIA THE TINY window of the phone screen, I can tell my little sister is bouncing in her seat. I brace myself for the incoming Spanish Inquisition. I prepare myself for the inevitable and wait for her to start peppering me with questions.

"So what are you going to name him?" She asks, wasting no time, her face wreathed in a giant grin.

I thought for sure she was going to ask me again if I'm happy. She still feels guilty about staying at Notre Dame instead of transferring closer.

"I haven't decided yet," I smile back.

"Listen, Big Brother of Mine. Don't make it something lame. It needs to have character and reflect his personality," she sternly informs me.

"Pipsqueak, you do realize we're talking about a guinea pig."

"Yes, I'm aware. But he'll be the first pet you've ever had. Your little sidekick," she pauses for a second. "He needs to have a name that matches his awesomeness. He's going to be your only company."

I push my hair off my forehead and wink. "About that..."

She squeals. "You met someone?" She claps her hands together delightedly.

"Well, not exactly. I'm still trying to convince her to give me the time of day."

She gives me one of her looks. The one that says, you're an idiot if you doubt your charm. "I've seen how you are around women, remember?"

"She's unlike any woman I've met."

"Holy crap," her eyes light up. "I never thought I'd see you pining over a woman."

"Who said I was pining?" I scowl.

"You are so pining. Bro, I never thought I'd see the day," she breaks into uncontrollable laughter.

I sigh resignedly. "So what do you want to know? I may as well give you ammunition now – otherwise you'll be insufferable," I grouse.

"Hello, that's my job as your sibling. To give you shit," she narrows her eyes on me. "It's our love language."

She's right. It's the way we show each other we're there no matter what. That we'll show up for each other. That we won't let anyone come between us. My bond with my sister is the strongest one in my life. I would run into a burning building to save her cat, Bob Marley. Even though he looks at me like I'm a flea far beneath his notice. Even though I'm allergic to cats.

"It is," I agree. "Where do I start?"

"Just tell me what she's like and how you met," she props her chin in her hands.

"Her name is Sarah Fraser and --" I'm interrupted by another squeal.

"The Sarah Fraser?" she breathes in awe.

"What do you mean the Sarah Fraser?"

"She still holds a ton of records she set in college. She's one of the best women's soccer players of all time."

"Yes, that Sarah Fraser. But she's retired now."

"Yeah, I heard she retired after the shooting," she somberly replies.

"Shooting?" I carefully ask. "What shooting?"

She rolls her eyes at me. "How do you always do such a half-ass job of googling someone? If I know you, you probably went down a YouTube rabbit hole and watched forty-seven thousand soccer videos and didn't bother re-searching anything else about her."

She's not wrong and I can't dispute her, so I just raise a brow.

"The shooting that ended her career. She wasn't hurt, but I think someone close to her was. She just disappeared after that. The guy that opened fire in the bar was someone who'd been stalking her."

"No wonder she hates crowds," I mutter.

"Yeah, can you blame her? And no wonder she's decided to live her life in the middle of nowhere."

"You found all of this out by googling her? How'd you even know she lives here?"

"How do you not know that I thoroughly unearthed every detail I could find about Willow Creek when you told me you were moving there? When you told me you were moving there to establish a horse farm that would help kids like me?" She blinks rapidly against the tears in her eyes.

My eyes are wet too. "I just wish I could've been there for you."

"You're here for me now. What happened to us as kids wasn't your fault, and you've been the best brother any sister could ask for. I am the most well-adjusted socially awkward woman I know."

I smile ruefully. "You're going to give someone a helluva ride one day."

"Only because you taught me to ask for what I deserve."

She's come so far. I assumed her guardianship as soon as I turned eighteen. She was a skinny kid with an overbite and a chip on her shoulder like the world's biggest pinata full of sour patch kids and lemonheads, distrustful of everyone and completely shut off from her peers. Determined to believe the worst.

She was fifteen and she'd never had a decent pair of shoes, someone to play double dutch with at recess or someone to share popcorn with over a matinee. Until me. I'd never had those things either until we were finally together again. Thinking about how much she means to me makes my throat tight.

"So, how did the two of you meet?" she prompts.

"She's one of Taren's best friends. We met when her three-legged race partner stood her up."

"You were in a three-legged race, and I missed it?" she asks, wide-eyed.

"I was. And we fell. And then we lost to a pair of eight-year-olds I predict will be our future overlords."

"That is hilarious. You are so competitive, I bet you were like a little grumbly lion cub."

"I do not grumble," I protest.

"Whatever, you would win the gold medal for grumbling if it was actually an Olympic category."

"You're the only person I know that insists I have this problem."

"Everyone else is just too intimidated to tell you. I bet this woman will be the opposite of intimidated."

"If she ever lets me close enough, I'll let you know," I wryly predict. "Do you have a lot of reading for tonight?"

"Ugh. Don't remind me. It's fascinating, but boring at the same time. Bioengineering models."

"That sounds absolutely fascinating," I deadpan.

"You're hopeless. I think you would actually find it interesting. I'm going to make you read my dissertation over Thanksgiving break," she warns.

"I look forward to it," I do. But only because it's something she's passionate about. I'll grin and bear it.

"No, you don't. Not really. But that's okay. Because next Wednesday when we talk you're going to make it up to me by letting me know what my nephew's name is."

"Your nephew?" I choke out.

"Yes. That little spotted guinea pig in your lap," she shakes her head at me and blows me a kiss. "Night, Big Brother."

"Night, Pipsqueak," I hang up and look down at the ball of fur lazing against my stomach. He looks like a pair of wire-rimmed glasses should be perched on the edge of his snout. I had to wear a pair just like them when I played Woodrow Wilson on the school's President Day Pageant when I was in the fifth grade. Maybe the twenty-eighth POTUS should be his namesake. Especially since I had to remember the Fourteen Points speech at the age of ten and it was one of the only times I can remember both of my parents watching me proudly from the row of folding chairs that stretched across the gymnasium. They weren't big on school functions because of the transient nature of Dad's job.

We were living in a really nice trailer outside Ft. Worth and Dad was training some stakes horses for an oil baron. The community was the kind that took care of its own – bringing you casseroles when they heard you were under the weather and offering to water your flowers if you were going out of town. The teachers were nice too, or at least it felt like they weren't as judgmental as they were in some of the places we'd lived. And the school librarian would sneak me books to take home to Ellery.

So maybe that little slice of my growing up, a slice I forgot about until I moved to Willow Creek, is something I should memorialize. My stint as a mini-Woodrow Wilson was one of the last times I saw my parents out in public together before Dad was thrown to his death. One of the last times we were a happy family. Woodrow Wilson it is, W.W. for short.

I'm bleary eyed this morning, desperate for coffee. I feed my new best friend and he snuffles my hand. I give him a final pat on the head and fortify myself. I forgot to pick up pods for the Keurig on the counter, and if I want to be a functioning adult it looks like I'll be harassing my new neighbor sooner rather than later.

I walk through the border of white pine and spruce and find the woman who had a very prominent role in my dreams last night standing on her balcony overlooking the lake. Her hands are curled around a mug the size of a small island. Or maybe even an entire archipelago. I'm praying it holds strong coffee instead of herbal tea, and that she needs the smell of fresh grounds to jumpstart her morning too. At least then we'd have that in common, and maybe she'll take pity on my inability to function without it.

She gives me a look of disbelief as I stroll towards her, rubbing her knuckles over one eye like she's trying to dispel a hallucination.

"How arc you here?" She groans. She's looking at me with more than a hint of accusation. As if she thinks I connived my way into occupying the space beside hers. Which I didn't, not really. I will admit that being this close to her sooner than I expected is even better than the realized dreams of my eight-year-old self when I discovered a really cool temporary tattoo in the bottom of my Cracker Jack box. It's like the feeling I got when I popped three wheelies in a row on my bike, showing off for Hannah Squires. Before I went sailing over the handlebars and broke my nose. Yeah, that reminder of what happens when I let the daredevil on my shoulder take control is all I need to rein myself in. I'm not going to let myself short-circuit this opportunity.

"I'm renting the cabin beside yours," I calmly inform her.

"How did I not know about this? I mean I knew there was someone over there when I saw the truck. But why didn't anyone see fit to inform me that you'd be my new neighbor?" One hand lands on her hip and she glowers at me like I'm the demon spawn of Satan.

"Well Dex owns it. And Zane knew. I'm surprised Taren didn't tell you."

She looks perturbed at that revelation. Like Taren's had plenty of chances to relay such important information and chose not to tell her. Like she's wondering why Taren didn't tell her and planning vengeance. "Well Dex owns mine too, and he didn't warn me. And Taren didn't either," she grumbles. "What do you want?"

I coast my hand through my hair. "I forgot to pick up coffee last night," I sheepishly admit, and give her a hound dog grin. I'm begging her to take pity on me and hoping it works. There are very few people who can resist my grin.

She arches a supercilious brow. Okay, maybe she's one of those rare people who has no trouble resisting my grin. "And now you're standing on my doorstep begging for handouts. That's so cliché. I suppose you think all you need to do is flash that smile and you'll get whatever you're asking for."

I can't tell if she's teasing or not. I'm betting she's not. That would track. She doesn't seem like someone who would be susceptible to my grin or persuaded by it. If I wasn't so desperate for my morning wake-up call I'd admire her for giving me shit this early. "Please take pity on me, Fierce Girl. I can't face all that teen angst without caffeine."

"I thought you didn't have to be there until this afternoon for practice. That gives you plenty of time to run into town for groceries and mentally prepare yourself. I don't think I need to take pity on you."

"I'm teaching now, too," I confide. "And I need that cup of coffee to function like a semi-normal adult."

Her eyes narrow again. Like this is another essential piece of information no one deemed necessary to tell her. "You are?" she asks me incredulously. "How? Last I heard, you didn't exactly have the credentials."

"I'm not bad at applied mathematics. It was my minor. And the other math teacher, Ms. Gershwin, is out on unexpected FMLA. Principal Greene pushed my paperwork through so I could sub as well as coach."

She seems flabbergasted. "Of course he did," she rolls her eyes. "Why would you be willing to do that? You don't seem like the knight in shining armor saving the village from Mordor type. I mean, besides the whole, saving the town with your investment thing. This will require you to actually climb down into the trenches, and you strike me as the kind of guy who would be opposed to that."

"What can I say? Maybe I have a soft spot for hobbits. And I can't do anything with the farm until construction is finished. So, will you take pity on me?" I ask again.

"Fine," she turns on her heel. "But don't think you're going to make a habit of it. Mornings are my time for finalizing my lesson plans and getting into the proper mindset to face '*all of that teen angst*', as you call it. I don't like being interrupted," she whirls back to face me and puts a hand on her hip. "And wait a second, are you calling me a hobbit? I know for a fact I don't have to shave my toes."

"You're definitely not a hobbit," my eyes roam over her like she's the last bit of tiramisu at my favorite Italian restaurant.

She tugs her silky robe tighter around her waist. "Then what am I?" she challenges.

"You make me remember why I had a thing for Eowyn. All of that bristling and smoldering," I admit. "A woman who can take care of herself and knows what the pointy end of a sword is for. I mean she faced down a huge orc by herself."

"Hmmm. I would definitely face down an orc with the pointy end of a sword. I can't stand bullies. The Eowyn obsession surprises me - most men have a thing for Liv Tyler as Arwen," there's speculation in her gaze, like I moved to the head of the class. "Because your answer isn't typical you can come in the side door – it opens into the kitchen."

I want to pump my fist in the air.

She disappears and I stroll around the side of the house. There's a small patio with a sliding screen door. I'm raising my hand to knock when she slides the door out of the way. And I realize with agonizing clarity that she unbelted her robe and she has on nothing but a cropped tank top that's sliding off her shoulder and threadbare cotton boxers underneath it. I gulp and drag my eyes away from the beguiling curve of her shoulder and the endlessly entrancing length of her legs. I ignore the way the frayed edges of the boxers hug her succulent thighs. I grimace and close my eyes, trying to marshal my thoughts. I repeat the rosary at least twenty-five thousand times and try to think about the nature documentary I watched on the life of slugs. Anything to curb my attention elsewhere.

She ignores my preoccupation, waves toward the Keurig on the counter and then toward the little breakfast nook in the corner. "I don't have any creamer, so it really will be like fueling yourself for the day."

"I drink it black anyway. It matches my soul."

"Point proven," she smirks, like she never doubted the darkness of my soul, that it was a foregone conclusion. Apparently she really does believe I'm the demon spawn of Satan. Or Sauron. I can work that into my fantasies. She reminds me of a certain sexy vampire slayer with her snark, her long blond hair and her mesmerizing blue eyes.

"Do you always get up this early?" All her bristling energy signals that she's an early riser.

"Yes. I do yoga first thing."

An image of her in Ubaya Konasana floods my brain, and I have to think about slugs again. "Makes sense," I mumble in response.

"There's bread on the counter if you want to make yourself some toast. I'm going to go take my shower and finish getting ready."

"Okay," I don't say anything else because I'm consumed by the thought that she'll soon be naked somewhere in this house.

It's about an hour and a half later, and I'm grabbing my helmet when there's a frantic knocking at my door. I swing it open and there she is.

"Fancy seeing you again so soon." Our morning meeting should have filled her Blake quota for the day. I wouldn't exactly call her a fan.

I receive a disgusted eye roll in response. "My truck won't start. I'm pretty sure it needs a new alternator, but I can't put it in until this weekend. Can I ride with you?"

I'm not even surprised that she was able to diagnose the problem and knows how to fix it herself. This woman is fifty thousand kinds of competent and it's the biggest turn-on. "If you don't mind hopping on my bike, you can. And if you change into jeans."

Her face blanches. "Motorcycles aren't my kind of cat-nip," she admits as she bites her lip and nervously brushes her hair behind her ears. "What happened to the truck I saw in your driveway when you moved in?"

I step toward her and cradle her cheek in my hand before she can scoot away. "It was a rental. I promise I'm very careful, and always drive defensively. Maybe you just haven't experienced motorcycles with the right person."

"You don't own a car?" She asks, looking up at me with those baby blues full of trepidation.

"I do, but the bike is ready now and it's going to be the perfect weather for a ride," unable to resist the impulse, I drop a gentle kiss on her lips. "I'll make sure you're safe," I murmur.

She shakes her head, like she's in a daze, and then looks down at her toes in embarrassment. "I don't like motorcycles. They've always scared me."

I'm surprised at her confession. I never thought this woman would admit to fear. "I promise I'll be extremely conscientious of my precious cargo," I'm still cupping her cheek in my palm, and I'm surprised she hasn't wriggled away.

She exhales loudly and squares her shoulders. "Ok. Let's do this. I'll meet you out front on ten minutes."

Chapter 7

Sarah

I CAN'T BELIEVE BLAKE Armitage is my new neighbor. I can't believe he cupped my cheek in that broad, calloused hand and gave me a kiss for reassurance. I can't believe

I was off my game enough for him to give me a kiss of reassurance. It was nothing but an inconsequential peck on the lips, a barely there whisper. But I felt its tingle at the base of my spine. I felt it oozing through my veins like slow-moving lava, porous and sweet. I should've stepped beyond his reach or protested when he did it. But I didn't. And now it feels like I crossed an invisible line and invited him to cross it with me. I don't want to give him the impression that he can take liberties.

So now, despite all the warning bells and against my better judgment, I'm straddling a motorcycle behind him. I'm not even going to contemplate how this is going to fuel the local rumor mill. Or mess with my peace of mind and solitude. I have an inkling that he won't stay confined to his side of the tree line. I have this feeling that my capitulation was an open invitation to borrow coffee, or sugar, or matches, or whatever else he can think of to sneak past my defenses. Like the raccoon that thinks my trash can is his own personal pantry.

I'm sure the whole town already knows we're neighbors, and when news of our shared ride to the high school gets around the speculation about our nocturnal activities is going to blow the roof off. Especially since I've never brought a date to a school event. When I need that kind of release I go all the way to the city. It's much easier to find a no-strings attached one night stand via a Tinder hook-up. It's not the kind of connection that encourages in-depth conversation.

He told the truth – he really is a conscientious driver. He takes every curve with an excess of caution, and I feel much safer than I thought I would plastered against his back, my arms around his waist. He had an extra helmet he insisted I wear, and I'm determined to be grateful for the sweat-soaked mash of hair it will leave behind.

The landscape spooling past us, emerging as the morning mist lifts from the hills, makes me breathless despite my fear. The scent of his cedary aftershave, and the hint of amber that always seems to cling to his clothes, curls around me as I bury my nose between his shoulder blades and inhale.

When we pull into the school parking lot, we're greeted by a dumbfounded crowd of students and teachers. He holds the bike steady for my dismount. He had the foresight to make sure I changed into pants and I'm singing hallelujahs as I swing my leg over. He insisted I'd be grateful for the switch. I'm just now reluctantly agreeing with him. If he hadn't intervened I'd be standing here with the wind whipping my skirt up like a Marilyn Monroe montage, revealing my black thong to the entire staff and student body. Instead, I have on a pair of dark denim jeans that may as well be painted on. I notice how his gaze strays as I hand him the helmet so I can shake my hair out. He's still sitting there, watching me. I put my hands on hips. "Thank you, Mr. Armitage, for the ride. It wasn't what I expected."

He removes his own helmet and hangs it from the handlebars, peering at me from behind the sweaty mess of his own hair. It waves around his face, darker caramel instead of honey now because of the sweat soaking those golden strands. He puts down the kickstand and swings off the bike, grabbing his nape in one hand, pulling a dark band from around his wrist and twisting it all up into his usual man-bun. "You'll always be safe with me, Fierce Girl," he steps closer and pushes my damp curls behind my ear. "And I told you to call me Blake," he gruffly admonishes.

"One motorcycle ride does not put us on a first name basis on school grounds," I pertly reply. I'm not going to call him by his first name. I let my guard down too soon when we met. I'm going to blame it on the backward baseball cap and his day-old scruff. If I revert back to that momentary lapse in judgment it'll only make it look like there really is an open invitation to cross the tree line any time the urge hits him. He's way too much of a threat to my equilibrium to encourage. Raccoon meet trashcan.

"Then decide on my nickname already. Whatever. But no more Mr. Armitage. You make me feel like you're going to break out my middle name at any second. Either call me by my first name or come up with whatever pet name you're going to bestow on me."

I grin. "I would call you by your middle name if I knew it. I like having that effect on you. It keeps you on your best behavior. And who said it was going to be a pet name? It's not going to be a pet name. The nickname I finally choose will be more like an insult," I'm only half-teasing. If it's more like an insult it will be easier to keep him at arms' length.

He stalks toward me until we're standing toe to toe, the tension crackling between us. "I might tell you my middle name if you promise to cook me breakfast after," he silkily promises.

My face flushes the vibrant red of a Roma tomato. He means breakfast the morning after. "Are you propositioning me?" I ask in disbelief. The man has no shame.

"If you come up with an insulting nickname, you're asking me to show you something besides my best behavior," his eyes bore into me. "Do you want to be forced to rap me across the knuckles with your ruler, Fierce Girl?" he challenges.

"I want to rap something," I bite out. And then I can't help blushing again because I'm embarrassed at what I just revealed. With a start I realize that we're the focus of the whole parking lot's rapt attention. I don't know whether they think it's a train wreck or a telenovela, but we have them mesmerized. I even hear a couple of whistles. I don't think they can hear our subdued conversation, but I don't want to give them any more fodder for speculation. "Ugh. Now you've made us the center of attention and singlehandedly managed to provide grist for the gossip mill," I whirl away, determined to appear completely at ease despite my discomfort. I see him slide his sunglasses on in my peripheral vision, and I'm sure it's because he's trying to hide the fact that he's ogling me as I walk away. He makes me feel like we're acting out the Olivia Newton John and John Travolta dynamic in *Grease*.

The hubbub I heard coming from the teacher's lounge is abruptly silenced when I walk through the door. Great, queue up the rumor mill. Now we're the newest topic of conversation here as well. I pointedly ignore the cluster of my colleagues nursing their morning coffee and stride toward the half full carafe. Once I'm holding it like an anchor, I pivot toward them, bracing myself for the worst.

"Sooo...," prompts the new Home Ec teacher.

"So what?" I counter, as I turn around and lift the cup to my lips. I'm not going to cave and satisfy their curiosity that easily. But I can feel my hands shaking. I hate that I'm in this situation. It's because he looks like he does, and the whole town has decided he needs to wife up. They're all vying for the position, and now I'm in their crosshairs.

"So what's the deal with you and our newest eye candy?" The Home Ec teacher asks a little defiantly. It's clear from her posture and the jut of her jaw she thinks I've poached on territory she already staked out.

"Nothing. We're neighbors," I state matter-of-factly.

"That doesn't explain the cozy motorcycle ride," sneers the Spanish teacher.

"It does if my truck wouldn't start, and I didn't want to be late. Apparently he doesn't own a vehicle," I'm angry at the assumption I hear in her tone, and I want to make it clear that I sought his help because I had no other choice. Not because I've thrown my hat in the ring to be the next lion-tamer.

"Yes, he does," pipes up the Environmental Sciences teacher. "I saw him flashing around in a Maserati a couple of weeks ago. I thought my husband was going to stroke out he was salivating so hard at the sight of it."

The other two are still glaring at me, like I used my wiles to obtain a tandem motorcycle ride.

"Well, I obviously didn't know about the Maserati he has hidden," I grimace. "Because if I'd known about it, I would've insisted on it instead of the motorcycle. Much more dignified," I conclude.

"And just as sexy," observes the math teacher. She's looking at me like I need a head transplant. "But you don't really care about that, do you?"

I vehemently shake my head.

"Huh. Maybe that's why you're the only one who seems to have snagged his attention – because you're playing hard to get. Maybe that's what we all need to do," she observes excitedly.

The possibility of Blake Armitage being cockblocked from the pursuit of easily acquired, no strings sex, makes me happy. "Maybe that is what all of you need to do."

They immediately bend their heads to conspire, and I want to rub my hands together in glee. Maybe he'll bestow that smoldering gaze on someone else for a change.

The hours creep by with agonizing slowness. I spend my lunch break grading the dismal pop quiz showing from first period. When the final bell rings, I stretch with a sigh of relief. Today is the last day of tryouts. I still haven't found my sweeper, but one of the sophomores who an-chored the relay team last year is demonstrating her skills today.

The boys' team is already at the other end of the field, doing front leg kicks and jumps. Blake is yelling from the sidelines, hands on his hips, the whistle between his teeth. I ignore him because I don't need more Captain Von Trapp stern brunch daddy fodder for my imagination. He's wearing a pair of basketball shorts today and a black tank that's sticking to his skin in the drowsy afternoon heat of early September. I look away because I refuse to let him see me drooling over the slide of sweat down his bicep or the weirdly erotic sight of his bare knees.

The girls are glancing covertly over, trying to disguise the fact they're fascinated by the new coach and his train-ing techniques.

"Coach Fraser, who will get the good field for the open-ing game?" Queries my forward, Alejandra.

"Since we had a winning season last year, it should be us." My goalie Michaela decisively observes.

"It should be. And it had better be," I agree. Common sense would dictate that we get first pick. But unfortu-nately, I know how these things tend to not work in favor of the girls' team. I've had to fight tooth and nail to get adequate funding for our uniforms – even though we've put the town on the map by going to state three years running. We're the best sports team the school has – and the most underappreciated.

I'm going to have to approach my nemesis and demand we get the use of the field free of divots for our first home game. I doubt the boys' team will be in top form by then because it's only two weeks away.

"I want everyone to focus on footwork with stepovers while I have a word with my colleague," I inform them. "Alejandra, can you monitor and guide anyone who needs it?" She shakes her head eagerly. She has amazing footwork, and I know she loves helping her teammates improve their skills. My conversation with Armitage should be straightforward, but I notice my players nudging each other in anticipation. I throw my shoulders back determinedly, and march to the other side of the green.

He must have eyes in the back of his head because he swivels around when I'm about six feet away.

"How may I be of assistance, Coach Fraser?" He asks around the whistle still clenched between his teeth.

"We need to decide which field we're going to use for the first scrimmage in two weeks."

He drops the whistle. "Well obviously, the boys' team has the bigger fan base. So we'll be using this one."

I can't tell if he's purposefully antagonizing me. His smile seems ironic. "That's such crap," I retort. "You may have a bigger fan base, but you know your team sucks compared to ours." He knows I'm right. And that my team should get the field that has had better maintenance because they deserve it. I'm trying to build the confidence of my team, so I'm not willing to budge. "I think we should see which of us can land a goal."

"You want to kick off against me?" He smirks in disbelief. At least I think he's smirking. He could be teasing me. There's no way he hasn't been given an earful of my history by now.

"Sure. I'll even let you stand closer to give you the handicap."

"No. You're pretty confident in your abilities, Fierce Girl," his eyes rake over me. "Are you sure you want to give me the advantage of a handicap?"

"Yep," I scoff. He won't know what hit him. "I could do this hobbled and with one leg tied behind me."

"Fine. We'll do it your way. Even steven. As soon as practice is over."

Now I can't wait to kick his arrogance down his throat. Practice cannot be over soon enough.

I stroll back over to my players, a tingle of anticipation like lightning down my spine at showing this alpha male I have his number.

"Ok, team. We'll know by tomorrow which field we'll be using," they pump their fists in the air. "But no matter which field we end up on, our opponents don't stand a chance."

My instincts about the sprinter were on point, and I now have first- and second-string sweepers. As I call out the names and positions, there's a lot of smiling and a few tears. "For those of you who didn't make first or second string this time, I still want you on my intramural teams. The more opportunities you have to practice your footwork, the better." This clears up the tears somewhat, and they shake their heads in agreement.

His whole face lights up with a blazing grin when I walk up with the soccer ball in my hand. We've cleaned up the field and it's just us. He looks as eager as me. The constant zip of tension hovers palpably between us. It's heightened because we're both determined to win this contest of wills and skill.

"Let's get down to it, Fierce Girl," he prods.

His voice is low and rumbly on the quiet field. The sound makes me want to clench my thighs together. Like he's a sexy merman siren or something. An Aquaman who's also the Pied Piper. I lower my brows to convey my irritation. "Yes. Let's get down to it."

I still haven't come up with a nickname for him. I call him all kinds of things in my head. Like delicious. And temptation incarnate. And the biggest threat to my self-control I've ever met. All of which are completely inappropriate for casual conversation. Taren and Emma would never let me hear the end of it if they could read my mind.

We set up our kicks right beside each other. I guess he decided he didn't need the handicap.

Of course mine sails right into the net. His does not. He overjudges and it soars over the top of it.

I expect a temper tantrum at his failure. But instead, he just shrugs his shoulders. "Oh well. I figured there was a slim chance in hell of me besting you at this. I googled you and there are tons of YouTube videos of you out there from your NCAA days."

I laugh, both embarrassed and proud. "You googled me? And you were just trying to get under my skin earlier, questioning the wisdom of giving you a handicap?"

"Well, duh. I mean you did throw me to the ground within fifteen minutes of our first meeting."

I roll my eyes because now I know he's teasing me. "Which was an accident. We should have won that trophy." The trophy was a twenty-five-dollar gift card to Dairy Queen. Which I would have used to try at least four different Blizzards.

"I concede the better field to you. I'll even help drum up butts for the bleachers," he offers his hand for a polite shake.

I take it. But he doesn't shake it. Or let go. He just devours me with that intense gaze. "What are you looking at?" I challenge. He's making me self-conscious, and every inch of my skin feels like I'm going to spontaneously combust. Which I've never witnessed, even though I used to devour the stories in my sister's Ripley's Believe It or Not book about the phenomenon. Especially the one about the girl that burst into flame in the middle of the dancefloor.

"You. I'm always looking at you. I can't stop looking at you," he slides his thumb across my palm.

There are so many hornets buzzing through me right now it's like an ACDC or Trans-Siberian Orchestra concert is happening in my stomach. "Well, as we've discussed, I'm not interested."

"I'm determined to persuade you otherwise. Can we wager something over a game of darts?"

"Why darts? That's such a random choice," I suspect he suggested darts because he's much better at them than soccer.

"Because I'm good at them. Much better at them than I am at soccer."

Suspicion confirmed, and I'm not surprised my guess was correct. Even though he's not being an asshole about it, I can tell he doesn't often lose. It's been a harrowing but rewarding first week and I could really use a beer. "How about right now?" I ask impulsively. And being this impulsive is completely out of character for me. I wonder if I can blame my lapse of judgment on the gray sweatpants. Or the manbun trapped under the bill of his backwards baseball cap. Or his motorcycle and cliché leather jacket. Who am I kidding? I can just blame it on the whole sexy package. But even if I do that, I'm still not going to become a member of his giggling fan club. Wherever he eats lunch, he's surrounded by a gaggle of simpering women. Like preening Canadian geese marching across a busy intersection – completely oblivious of their surroundings. They act like moonstruck, giddy teenagers, silently screaming, *"Pick me! Pick me! I volunteer as tribute."* And it's not just because the ratio of single women to single men is two to one in our county. It's because he's so approachable and still a completely different species from the other prospects. He exudes Mufasa energy in a town that sometimes feels like it's full of ridiculously petty hyenas.

I never volunteer to engage in social situations. I strenuously avoid any interaction that has the whiff of a date. So I will never be one of his besotted hangers on. That would mean the pressure of disappointing someone, of making myself vulnerable to criticism. I don't know what prompted me to suggest spending more time with him. He's already impossible to resist and the hornets in my stomach have taken up permanent residence.

His whole face lights up at my spontaneous suggestion. "That would be great. Let's meet at Guy's."

Now I want to take it back. He looks more like a golden retriever ready to lick my hand than a lion surveying his kingdom. Too eager. Like I invited him to cross the tree line any time he wants. Even though I've kept my distance since the motorcycle ride. I tell myself I'm agreeing because Guy's Bar is my favorite place in town besides Cupcake on Main and our local Mexican restaurant. "You're on! I'll see you there in twenty minutes," I know there's a FIFA match tonight, and I'm looking forward to watching it with a tumbler of scotch.

Chapter 8

Blake

My eyes are glued to the door. She strolls in, still flushed and gorgeous from our competition. She seems more receptive toward me, and I'm nervous about jinxing it. I have to put my hand on my knee to keep my leg from jiggling up and down on the footrest of the bar stool. I feel like I just slid a note across my desk asking her to circle yes or no.

She notices me right away. My bar stool is turned almost completely around, and there's no way she can miss the way my eyes want to eat her up. So I shouldn't be surprised. She slides onto the stool beside me and gives me a sideways smile. "Your beer is getting warm," she chides. "Now that I'm here, why don't you drink instead of watching the door?" She gestures toward my half full draft.

"You're way more fascinating than this IPA," I don't bother correcting her assumption. I was fiendishly focused on the door and there's no way I can disguise it.

"Well, the Manchester United match playing behind you is the most interesting thing to me right now," she's determined to make me doubt my own appeal at every opportunity.

"When did your obsession start?" I'm curious if she's been following the sport as long as I have.

"It started in 1995, when I was eight. When Beckham's star was rising. My dad was a huge fan of the MU coach, Ferguson," she explains. "It's the one thing we had in common."

"That explains so much about your combative personality," I tease.

She rolls her eyes. "Whatever. I'm competitive, not combative. There is a huge difference. And you're one to talk. Even though you want me to think you're a graceful loser, you challenged me to a rematch of sorts. Which means that losing that kickoff to me stuck in your craw," she rests her chin in her hand. "Is it because you lost to a woman or because you can't stand to lose to anyone?"

My gaze moves over her. "If I'm going to lose to anyone, Fierce Girl, I'd prefer losing to you."

She shakes her head at my left-handed compliment.

We shout at the screen for the next thirty minutes. Just to be contrary and get under her skin, I cheer for Leeds. My cheering doesn't amount to a hill of beans. Of course Manchester wins. She whoops and whistles for a solid five minutes before she signals the bartender over.

"Do you want your usual celebration shot?" He asks her.

"Of course! But make it two," she replies enthusiastically. I'm assuming the second shot is for me and I'm curious, so I don't question it. I want to see what her special poison is.

He pulls out two glasses and the bottle of Drambuie from behind the counter.

"Wow. The OG scotch," I'm impressed by her fortitude. I've never tried it because I've imagined it tastes like Windex.

"It was my dad's favorite and it's become mine as well," she smiles wryly. "Should we toast to working together to bring visibility to our school's soccer program?"

"Sure. I like working with you," I agree.

We raise our glasses and clink them together.

We're staring at each other again. I don't think it's a faceoff, because her gaze tracks to my lips for half a second and she licks a single drop of whiskey from her own. If I hadn't been watching her just as intently, I would have missed that telling glance.

"Why were you staring at my lips, Fierce Girl?"

"None of your business, Arrogant Boy."

"I'm not a boy," I growl.

Her eyes flicker back to my lips. Like that growl wasn't the least bit menacing. "I'm well aware. I was intentionally trying to annoy you."

"So you've decided on my nickname?"

She props her elbow on the bar and rests her hand against her cheek. "I don't think so. That's way too tame for you. And speaking of which, I'm a woman, not a girl. So why that nickname for me?"

"Maybe I want to annoy you as well," I lean closer. "Maybe if you're busy being annoyed you won't be able to ignore me. You'll be so busy complaining about me, I'll never be far from your thoughts."

"You're kind of difficult to ignore," she scoots closer too. "And I'm not immune to your charms, I just don't have time for that right now," she props her chin in her hand and leans even closer. Like she's getting ready to confess her darkest secret or proposition me. I'm okay with either scenario. "I still don't think you'll end up being a permanent fixture in Willow Creek, and I don't do casual hook-ups with friends of my friends. Or co-workers," she turns away, restores the distance between us, and takes a sip of her highball. Completely undeterred.

"Why do you think I won't be a permanent fixture?" I challenge. I'm feeling something that hovers between angry and hurt. Why does she think I'm not invested in the farm or the charity I want to start here? Does she think I'm just a shallow playboy who makes decisions like that on a whim? I'm torn between being offended and wanting to dwell on the fact that she basically admitted she does have a set of casual hook-up circumstances and I don't meet her criteria.

She shrugs her shoulders. "Because you have buckets of money and you're used to globetrotting and dating swimsuit models and socialites and B list actresses. You're the kind of guy who likes silicone and manicured nails."

"You're making assumptions. I don't like either of those things. I don't like fake people and fake motives and contrived relationships. That's why I moved here. To get away from those things."

She rolls her eyes. "Such a hardship when you realize all that glitters isn't gold."

"I had to make every dime myself. I didn't have the luxury of a trust fund or an Ivy League education or all the connections everyone else in the shark pit had," I harshly retort. I close my eyes to calm my temper. She knows exactly which buttons to push to make me lose my cool. "My company's at the point now that I can step away. I don't need to babysit it or hold the reins as closely as I did ten years ago. I'm honestly thinking of selling," I confess. This is the first time I've admitted that to anyone but myself. Take that, Fierce Girl.

Her expression can only be described as patent disbelief. "You would voluntarily give all that up. On what looks like a whim, no less."

"And never look back. Yes. What exactly do you think I'm giving up? Life is more than piles of money that you never have time to spend, and people who would abandon you in a heartbeat if your black AMEX card got declined at lunch," I glower at her, because apparently she does think I'm a rich, shallow asshole fuckboy. And whatever attraction she feels isn't enough to overcome her assumptions about me.

"It sounds like a pretty pathetic existence," she's not even trying to disguise her sarcasm. "Don't get me wrong. I know that money doesn't buy happiness, but it can make it a lot easier to find it."

"I agree with you. That's why I'm here in Willow Creek – because money doesn't buy happiness," I finish my shot and try to compose myself again. "I'm surprised we're having such a philosophical discussion about the meaning of life over alcohol," I can't ever remember having such a deep discussion in a bar. Usually the people I come to places like this with are attracted to my looks, my money, or both. They're either with me to ensnare me or freeload off me. They know better than to insult me by casting aspersions on my character. The fact that neither of these things seems to be driving her just adds to my fascination. Even if it pisses me off.

"I don't mind making you uncomfortable with my observations," she grins. "My nickname in college was Sophocles, so this is what I thrive on. And if you're so determined to get to know me better, this is the perfect way for you to see inside my head," she raises her glass in a mock toast. "So do you just gobble up prime corporate real estate or do you pay attention to how your greed affects others?" She gestures for a refill of her highball.

"For your information, I make sure every corporate deal I make is counteracted by the deliberate construction of affordable housing to offset the consequences of gentrification," I don't reveal my charitable side to many people, but I can tell it's the only thing that'll obliterate my douchebag reputation in her eyes. "So, is our conversation going to become more abstract if we consume more alcohol?"

She sighs comfortably. "So, you do have a conscience," she observes. "And yes, possibly. You seem like you're open to deeper conversation, and it's been a long week. I need to unwind."

Okay, noted. Showing her I'm not an ogre was the right move and esoteric discussion is how she relaxes. "Why has it been a long week?"

She eyes me with apparent chagrin. "Well, you're part of it."

I look at her expectantly. Her breath leaves her chest in a big gust. "Ugh. Okay. I thought I would never have to have this conversation. That I could just bury it by avoiding you and my annoying little problem would go away."

"You do know we work together, right? How exactly did you plan on avoiding me? And your problem? I'm part of your problem?" I hope she's talking about what I think she's talking about. But it's been a long time for me as well, and maybe it's just wishful thinking on my part.

"My avoidance tactics have worked like a charm since that motorcycle ride two weeks ago. And you haven't dashed across the boundary of pines to bother me and ask for sugar or coffee," she shrugs. "That's made it a lot easier to conveniently ignore you and my attraction to you. To ignore the fact that it's been a really long time and my toy collection has been getting quite the workout. To ignore the fact that you have a partiality for wearing gray sweatpants, you wield a whistle with the cold precision of Captain von Trapp, and you apparently have a pet guinea pig named Woodrow Wilson."

I'm barely able to swallow the rest of my beer. So she was talking about what I hoped she was talking about. I have to be smooth about this. Hopefully she doesn't know I'm on the brink of losing my shit and telling her I am her willing servant. However she wants to use me. That I would gladly surrender my whistle to her and let her bark out all the commands. "Are you saying that whistles turn you on? That you've been having sex dreams, Fierce Girl? Sexy thoughts about me and all the things you want me to do to your body? And how'd you find out about my new best friend?" Ok, I sound much calmer than I feel.

"The girls in my AP Chemistry class were glued to your Instagram account. They were oohing and aahing over the picture of your pet dressed up like a pumpkin. I was intrigued, so I looked it up when I got home," she looks away, like she's bracing herself. "So yes, Arrogant Boy," she's looking me in the eyes again. "That's exactly what I'm saying. But all I'm going to do is talk about it."

There she goes calling me boy again. I want to bend her over the stool and show her exactly how much of a boy I'm not. "Wow, Fierce Girl. I can't believe you were Instagram stalking me."

"I wasn't stalking you, I was stalking your guinea pig," she corrects.

"Should I be afraid you'll creep across the property line in the middle of the night like a cat burglar and kidnap him?"

She scoffs. "No, I have a very territorial and possessive Husky. It's a one pet household."

"Okay, so you just like looking at pictures of Woodrow Wilson. What about me? Do you wish you had some pictures of me to look at? Don't you want to find out if my playboy reputation is deserved?"

"I'd probably look at them if someone shoved them in my face," she shrugs. "But doing anything more than looking at pictures or talking about it is an inconvenience," she sternly admonishes me.

"An inconvenience how? As in now is not a convenient time? Or there will never be a convenient time?" Fingers crossed it's the former and not the latter.

She shakes her head at me. "As in there will never be a convenient time."

Okay, so she just crushed all my hopes and sent them away to curl up in a corner and die.

"I have a feeling you'd be like kryptonite. Pretty and sparkly but deadly," she continues.

Of course it was the latter and she just steamrolled over my fantasies. She's on her fourth whiskey. And her filter is completely dormant. The alcohol turned it off and I'm fascinated by her uncharacteristic teasing and blunt honesty. "At least you think I'm pretty. Do I sparkle like Edward?" Never in a million years would I want a woman to compare me to Edward Cullen, but I really want to hear more about her fascination with me.

"Oh, yeah. Very pretty. But off limits because you'd wreak havoc on my sanity. Just like Edward fucked with Bella and made her want impossible things," she twirls a lock of hair around her finger and bites her lip. "You are dangerous. And you're an unknown quantity."

"Well, technically the things Bella wanted weren't impossible since she eventually received them," I contradict.

This prompts a very extravagant eye roll.

"So what would make me a known quantity?" I need her answer.

"You're just passing through. You're the interim soccer coach, the substitute teacher. You're the guy with all the answers blowing in the wind, allergic to commitment and gun shy of putting down roots."

She's echoing her argument from earlier. Her assumptions about who I am and what I want are pissing me off. "We've already discussed this. Tonight as a matter of fact. I'm putting down roots here in Willow Creek. I don't know why you find that so difficult to believe."

She snorts in response. "Your constant repetition doesn't make it true."

"I'll prove it to you. There's no way you'll still refuse to believe that I'm staying."

I will prove it to her. Even if it means years of parent teacher conferences and giving up every single one of my Saturday mornings for soccer practices and helping her run the cider booth at the farmers' market. Zane let slip that she operates the register every Saturday morning in September and October, and no matter how tonight turns out, I'm ambushing her there tomorrow.

She huffs a laugh. "Bring it on, Arrogant Boy. I'm waiting with bated breath."

At least she just gave me the opportunity. I'll make her eat her words with my staying power. In more ways than one. "Are we still on for darts? Is that an acceptable boundary?"

"That depends on what the prize is for winning," her voice is full of speculation, and maybe innuendo.

"I've been wondering what your lips taste like," I drawl, intent on disrupting her calm.

"I've been wondering the same thing about you. So, no matter who wins, there will be a goodnight kiss. Maybe then I'll stop thinking about it," she holds out a hand for me to shake.

I don't want to shake her hand. I want to taste her. The bar is emptying out because it's after eleven and there's no band playing tonight, but there are still too many witnesses. But the dartboard is finally free. "So best out of three? As in we each shoot our three darts one time, and whoever has the highest combined score wins?"

"Yeah, that works for me," she agrees. "We don't have to toss a coin because I don't mind if you shoot first. I need to objectively assess your skills, so I'll know what I'm up against."

Chapter 9

Sarah

HE HOLDS HIS ARM at a perpendicular, extremely professional almost right angle. It's slightly intimidating, and I
can already tell he's much better at darts than soccer. Al-

though our match wasn't exactly fair. According to Zane, he was pretty good in college, but didn't have the dedication to go professional. Whereas I played professionally in Europe after graduation. I wonder if he knows that. I wonder how much research he's done on me, how deep his interest goes. If his interest is at the level of obsession yet.

"So you look like you know what you're doing," I observe.

"Well, yeah," there's a little vee between his brows, like I confuse him. Like I'm a Rubik's Cube and the solution that's supposed to work isn't working. Like the reds and the blues will never line up or perfectly sync, even if the green and yellow sides are done. Like he's trying to figure me out and keeps getting thrown for a loop.

"There was a ninety-nine percent chance you weren't exaggerating the superiority of your dart moves to your kicking skills," I lament.

"You're basically telling me my kicking game is shit," he chuckles and runs his free hand down his face. His expression is halfway between awe and disbelief. "Well, you have every right to be conceited about your kicking skills. And you're right about my dart moves – I wasn't exaggerating. The tournaments I won my sophomore year of college provided the seed money for my first investment."

So he's kind of an entrepreneurial prodigy. "So you're a darts shark and a self-made multi-millionaire?"

"I like hearing you call me a shark," he grins and lets the dart fly. And of course he hits the bullseye. Right smack-dab in the center.

"Huh. Maybe I know what your nickname is now," so I won't be able to distract him because it's probably impossible to distract him from darts. And most likely pointless. I strongly suspect his teasing demeanor hides a scary level of competence and focus. My dart skills are light years away from his. They're deplorable in comparison. But I'm nothing if not competitive, so I'm going to give it my best effort. And even though I try to hold my arm just like he did, at an intimidating perpendicular angle, and even though I take a deep breath and exhale as I let go of the dart, it doesn't land where I want it to. I shake my fist at the dart quivering in the outer ring, just under the number five.

He can't hold back his laughter. "Irate at an inanimate object. Maybe you shouldn't have had that whiskey. Now I know the secret to lowering your defenses and denting the image of your perfection."

"For your information, whiskey only enhances my mental acuity," I loftily inform him.

"Not sure I believe that you're the exception to the rule. You'd be the first person I've ever met who's immune to the way whiskey leaches brain cells."

I'm suddenly the object of his laser focus. I stumble as I step aside. He catches me, rights me. Our arms brush, and I even feel his elbow slide along some side boob when he moves up to make his second shot. I feel the goosebumps rise over every inch of my skin. "Well, I am the exception," I belatedly, lamely retort.

His second dart lands in the bullseye. "Aced it again."

"Yeah, Shark is your new nickname," I grimace. No matter how much my competitive spirit rises to the occasion, I know when to admit to myself that I'm going to lose. And I hate losing. Even though we agreed that no matter who won we would be kissing. It's not the prize. It's the principle. I still focus like I'm wielding a poison arrow against a battlefield full of orcs. This time my dart lands just under the ten. I throw up my hands in frustration.

"Not everyone is good at every single thing," he reminds me unnecessarily.

I sigh. "I know that. But that doesn't stop me from being competitive. Even if I'm complete shit at it."

He tilts my chin up. "You're still perfect."

"I thought you said the whiskey ruined my perfection," I remind him.

"I lied," he's looking at me the same way he did when he found out I was afraid to get on a motorcycle with him. It's the same look he had when he kissed me gently and said he'd make sure I was safe. When he steps up beside me this time, the touch isn't casual. He deliberately throws his arm over my shoulders, and clasps me to his side. He hits the bullseye a third time. He doesn't even need his second arm for balance or leverage or whatever. His competence is annoying. And very tempting.

I move away from him slightly. "I'm not going to give up. Even though I don't have a snowflake's chance in hell of beating you."

"I would expect nothing less," his gaze is full of admiration and heat and longing. I think he would pull me down to the floor with him and roll around in the disgusting sticky residue that seems to cling to the linoleum of every bar floor, if he thought he could get away with it.

"Well, unlike you, I think I need both arms. And I need every advantage, so I know I at least won't miss the dartboard completely."

He steps away with obvious reluctance.

I do try my best. But a darts professional I'm not. This time my dart lands on the triple ring, under the twenty. I start jumping up and down. "Yes! Isn't that sixty points? Obviously my mental and physical acuity are not affected by whiskey," I try to look down my nose at him.

He just laughs. "Yes, that's sixty points. So your grand total score is seventy-five. Half of my total score of one hundred and fifty. Maybe a regular date with darts will hone your skills."

"Don't rub your prowess in," I laughingly admonish. "And does that mean you're asking me out on an actual date? What makes you think I'll accept?"

"You don't have to give me your answer now. I think you should wait until after the goodnight kiss. You should have an appreciation of all the skills in my arsenal so you can make an informed decision," he delivers this observation in a teasing tone, but I can tell he's serious.

I could be coy, but I decide that's not how I'm going to respond. "Yes. I need a full appreciation of your skills. But that's still not going to change my opinion. I'm convinced you're kryptonite. A sparkly, Edward version, but still kryptonite," I make sure he can see the heat leaking from my eyes as they greedily roam over him. Like he's the whole meal. Not just a luscious snack. A meal I want to sop up the way I use biscuits to sop up gravy. And not just any biscuits. The flaky, buttery kind my grandmother used to make using her granite ware bowl. The kind that she used to make without a recipe. The kind that made every meal a divine experience. Maybe I need to follow the advice I gave Taren about Zane. Maybe I need to chase my own orgasms. Even if he's nothing but kryptonite. Maybe then

I'll stop thinking about biscuits and religiously comparing them to sex.

"Then I'm driving you home. I only had one beer and a shot. And it's not like it's out of my way," he's regarding me with single-minded determination. He will brook no argument.

"And just leave my car here?" I still need to push the envelope.

"The gossip mill is already spinning like a hamster on a wheel so leaving your car here overnight isn't going to affect it one way or another," he chucks me under the chin. "I'll drop you off in the morning to pick it up. I'm assuming you scheduled Saturday morning practice as well?"

"I did," I want to call him out for being presumptuous. But there's no point, because I guess it makes sense that we both have Saturday practice scheduled the weekend before our first game. I saw his motorcycle in the parking lot. But I'm more excited than scared to climb behind him.

The streets are quiet and feel deserted for a Friday night. There's only the rumble and purr of the motor beneath us, and the weight of my arms around his waist as I inhale the spice of his cologne.

When he pulls into my driveway and shuts off the engine, I slide off before he can help me. I jog up the steps and jiggle my key in the lock. He follows me, and I know he can tell I'm questioning the wisdom of a kiss. What was I thinking? Supposedly curiosity killed the cat. I turn around to give him a peck on the cheek. Completely chickening out on our deal because suddenly the thought of kissing him, of having him disrupt my world is more than I can handle. Before I can lift my face to his, he dips down and kisses the corners of my eyes, one at a time. They flutter closed and I feel the whisper of his breath against my lashes. His lips graze the upper curves of my cheekbones, and then drop to my own.

I don't know what I was expecting. But it wasn't this tender assault on my senses that makes me feel like a roman candle is exploding in my chest. It wasn't a butterfly kiss that makes it impossible to ignore the scent of amber and earth enveloping me. It wasn't a featherlight tethering of my wrists against the wood of the door, hard at my back because I'm slumped against it. He didn't have to push me against it. My mind must have conned my muscles into surrender. They've involuntarily dissolved into a puddle and the only thing holding me upright is the door. The sweep of his lips over my face is the only thing grounding me. Between the slivers of time that make up a handful of breaths, he becomes an anchor in a world that always seems to be spinning out of my control. There are no maybes or what-ifs to worry about in this moment, just here and now. He bestows a gentle parting kiss on my forehead. I'm expecting him to call me Buttercup and say "as you wish" at any second, because him kissing my eyelashes is a scene straight out of my most detailed Princess Bride fantasies. Maybe I should start calling him Dread Pirate Roberts.

He's obviously not a mind reader, because he doesn't channel my obsession. But the lock of hair falling into his eyes still reminds me of Wesley. I reach up and brush it aside and he turns his face into my touch, like he's seeking the last ray of sun.

"So that's how you say goodnight? I thought I was supposed to have dreams about you afterward," I want his mouth on mine. I'll be dreaming about him regardless, but I'm tired of wondering what his kiss tastes like. I may as well run toward the fire instead of away from it. When I'm around him, all the chaos in my head slows down. I don't want to examine that phenomenon too closely; I just know that's how it is.

"Is that a dare, Fierce Girl? Do you want me to show you I really can be your kryptonite?," he asks as he steps close again. This time, both of his hands curve around my face, bracketing it. His thumbs press my chin up and every detail of his rugged profile is swooping toward me in high definition. When his lips land on mine, it's almost anticlimactic.

The gentle persuasion of his earlier kiss is missing. He's edged past persuasion, into desperation and claiming territory. "I've thought of nothing but your lips for days," he confesses. His teeth graze the bow of my mouth, and he brushes his tongue across my lips, begging for entry. He doesn't have to beg; my mouth is already opening. I greedily nip his full bottom lip. Our tongues are tangling together, and I'm pressed against the door again. My hands are scrabbling at the soft give of his cotton t-shirt, lifting it just above his waistline so I can feel the heat of his skin against my palms. I'm really tempted to explore the happy trail I discovered when we tumbled to the ground in the middle of our race.

"Your hands are like hot little irons on my skin," he mutters, and pushes even closer. My arms are fully encircling him now and I wrench the shirt all the way to just below his shoulders. I wish we weren't shrouded in shadows, that I had a better view so I could examine his tattoos. I have one hand buried in his hair, unraveling it, and tugging him relentlessly toward my mouth, and my other one is plastered to the divot between his abs and his left hip. I sweep my palm down across the expanse of satin skin I bared, loving the feel of his back muscles tensing against my touch. I dance my fingers lightly across his nape before I entwine them in his sandy locks again, and I feel his whole-body shiver.

He gently grasps my wrists and steps back. "We have to stop, Fierce Girl," he rasps. "Or I'm going to rip your clothes off against this door and lick you so far into kingdom come you forget your name. And I have the feeling that you wouldn't even be able to look at me afterward, let alone kiss me again. So I'm going to wish you sweet dreams and be on my way."

I'm rendered mute, abashed by my hunger. The sheer confidence when he confessed he wanted to lick me into kingdom come. Gah. I'm going to picture that expression on his face when I reach for my toy tonight. And I'm going to need it, because I'm so turned on I'm crackling all over my skin. "Okay," I agree.

He must hear something in my voice because he dips down again until his forehead is touching mine. "I want to stay, Sarah. But that isn't what you need right now."

The fragile peace shatters just like that. And the edge of my arousal is instantly diffused. The fact that he has the unmitigated gall to assume he knows what I need makes me suddenly furious. "What I need? How would you know what I need, Blake? Don't fucking patronize me."

"I see more than you think I see, and I can be a patient man. I'm not patronizing you; I'm just making an observation."

"You're imagining things that aren't there. Good night. And you're making it really hard for me to pick a nickname that isn't an insult," I angrily whirl away.

He tugs on my hand and lifts it to his mouth. The gentle kiss soothes me against my will, but I don't want him to know that. I want, no I need, to hold onto my anger.

"Good night," he responds. "I hope you dream about me."

"Not likely," I retort. I slip in my door and slam it shut to the sound of his amused chuckle. I need to stay out of his orbit instead of circling closer.

Chapter 10

Sarah

EMMA AND I AGREED to help Taren run her stand at the farmer's market this morning. She picked me up because I plan on fixing the truck this afternoon. Hayes Orchard and Cidery is giving out samples of all the new batch releases that were such a big hit at the festival, and selling hot cider toddies, freshly canned apple butter and the cider donuts Emma whipped up. Because this is the first year of bottling, Taren and Zane are cutting corners any way they can. Emma and I volunteered as tribute in exchange for all the free cider we can handle. I relieved Emma around ten - as soon as I washed the sweat off from practice this morning. I'm running the register rather than handling the tastings and it suits me just fine. Less opportunity for small talk.

The crowd has moved on to the next booth, and I have a few minutes to catch up on my current read. I have our current book club read of the Pennyroyal Green series, *How the Marquess Was Won*, and Charybdis seems like a cat after my own heart. Prickly. Pretty much an avoider of contact with people who try to sneak past his defenses. He's just escaped, and Phoebe is scared and worried. I'm pretty sure the jealous, manipulative, petulant witch has something to do with it.

"Why do you have your nose stuck in a book on a gorgeous day like today?"

I would now know that voice anywhere. It ripples over me like I've been dipped in a vat of chocolate. After a match in Belgium once, my friends and I took a factory tour, and I was fascinated by the paddles whipping back and forth through the tubs full of what would become truffles and bonbons. His voice makes me feel like I'm drowning a little bit, being flipped back and forth, and frothing between those paddles. I don't like having my reading time interrupted, so that's what I'm going to focus on. Not the shivers that just cascaded from my nape to my spine when I thought about that kiss.

I tell myself I'm cringing. But it's not all cringing. He's not exactly an entirely unwelcome interruption. Mainly because I haven't stopped thinking about that kiss. Or the fact that he was a gentleman when he dropped me off this morning to pick up my truck from Guy's. His arrogance last night pissed me off, but I'm reluctantly letting go of my anger. I heave a great sigh. "I have my nose stuck in a book because we're between customers. And this book is unputdownable. Especially now that I'm at a crucial point where I need to know right this second what's going to happen next."

"You should be taking in the sights, not burying your nose in a book," his arms are crossed over his chest, the tight cut of his t-shirt making his biceps look impossibly large. And he's wearing his hat backwards again. And I can smell him from here...the slightest hint of shadowy cedar trees looming over the water on a cool morning. It makes me want to close my eyes and savor the feel of the water against my fingers as I park my kayak in the middle of the lake.

It's hard to be annoyed when it's like he dressed especially for me. I know he didn't. He seems like the laid-back kind of guy who still chooses his wardrobe based on the frat boy sniff test. He seems way too informal to be a millionaire with his own personal plane and pockets deep enough to save an entire town. Even though he looks scrumdillyumptious, I'm an unrepentant bookworm, and his comment irks me. "I need to stay here. I can't just go wandering off. The crowd ebbs and flows and we'll have more customers in a matter of minutes. And you should know by now that's not really my thing. So stop interrupting my precious reading time."

"There are a lot of reasons behind your "No". There's no way you can concentrate with everything that's going on around you," he scoffs, but there's teasing laughter in his eyes.

"Uhm, yes. Of course I can. I'm oblivious to everything around me when I get lost in a book."

"Fine, Fierce Girl. I'll let you win this one. But only because I can get that way too. Especially if it's true crime. Although the way Zane keeps hyping the library's romance book club, I think I'm missing out. Is one of those books what has your attention captivated so completely?"

"Yes. It's the seventh book in the series. It's about a lady's companion who unobtrusively captures the notice of an icy nobleman. So much so that he buys her a hat she's been coveting for months. And I have a premonition he's going to rescue her cat."

"So a cat rescue is a grand gesture guaranteed to win a woman's heart. Noted," he makes an invisible checkmark in the air. "Should I be reading this book too, so I can get tips on how to woo you? Or should I just watch that Courtship show that is advertising its ability to show women what Bridgerton would be like in real life?"

"Woo me? Please tell me you aren't serious. I'm the last person in this town who would be susceptible to your wooing," at least I want to believe I am.

"What makes you so sure of that, Fierce Girl? I could've sworn you were melting in front of your door last night. And I thought we agreed that your pathetic darts game needs improvement."

He looks way too self-satisfied.

"Maybe it's just been a long drought. Maybe any guy would've made me crave more. And why do I need to date you to hone my darts skills? Aren't there leagues or something?" I know there are leagues and that is probably a far wiser way to hone my skills. Then again, the only reason I want to hone my skills is so I can beat him. Or at least give him some real competition.

"So you admit you were craving more," his gaze on mine is like a heat-seeking missile.

I'm tempted to rub my forehead and erase the red laser beam. I just glare in response.

"The question is, would you have craved more from someone else? Say the bartender that was eyeing you up last night, or Coach Murray?"

I duck my head and glance away. So he can't see he's right. I seriously doubt I would have craved more from either of those men. Nothing against them, they just don't light up my nerve endings like the man standing in front of me. Or make me feel safe. Which is an even more concerning reaction.

"I'm right," he murmurs.

"What if you are? The fact that we have chemistry doesn't mean I'm going to date you." Dating him would be a disaster.

"So you've been thinking about it," he can't contain his smug grin. "You're getting ahead of yourself, Fierce Girl. Have I asked you out on a date?"

"Well, technically, no. But you heavily implied it last night. And just now when you reminded me of my abysmal darts skills."

He bends down. And then he's whispering in my ear. "Exactly. Technically, no I haven't. But that doesn't mean I don't dream about having those long legs wrapped around my waist. Or burying my face between them. But that's not really a date, is it?"

So. He's dreamed about the same things I have. That doesn't mean I'm giving in. Or letting him know for sure that his suspicions are right.

"You'll have to try a lot harder than that to get me to say yes to a date. What you're describing is more like scratching an itch than it is dinner and a movie."

He straightens and starts walking backwards. Wagging his finger at me. "Remember? Technically, I haven't asked you out yet. So what are you considering saying yes to?"

"You're insufferable."

"You may think I'm insufferable. But you also think I'm irresistible," he winks and saunters off like he doesn't have a care in the world. Like he didn't just issue the ultimate challenge.

Once he exits the booth, I twist around on the stool and see Emma watching me with a narrowed gaze, her arms crossed over her chest. "What have you been hiding from us, Sarah?"

"Ugh. I don't want to talk about it. I wouldn't even have this problem if you hadn't abandoned me the day of the three-legged race."

There's a flash of something like guilt in her eyes. "If I could've been there, I would've been there. But what does my absence have to do with this flirty side of you I've never seen?"

"He was your stand-in for the three-legged race. And we may have crashed to the ground when we were almost at the finish line. Which resulted in being tangled together and we may have had a moment," I explain in a rush. "But that was not flirting."

With every pronouncement, her eyes go wider. "A moment. You had a moment with the hot, but evil developer guy. And that was nothing but flirting."

"Yes. We had a moment. And I want to stop thinking about it," I growl and clench my hands in exasperation. "But it's really hard to forget when he shows up everywhere I go, and he looks like that and now I know what his kiss tastes like and I want to climb him like a tree. And since you're apparently not privy to the town rumor mill, you may as well know that he took me to school on his motorcycle earlier this week. And we may have been seen engaging in a friendly game of darts at Guy's."

"Why am I just now hearing about this? Especially the fact that you know what his kiss tastes like? Have I really been that oblivious, or are you just holding out on me?"

"A little of both," I sheepishly inform her. "In your defense, it is new. And recent. And embarrassing. He's a colleague. He's coaching the boys' soccer team. He's my next-door neighbor and he's seen me in my bathrobe."

"It's not like he's your boss, so I don't know why that's an issue. And I've seen your bathrobe. It's not some ratty, unattractive terry cloth monstrosity. If I remember correctly, it's a little silk thing that barely comes to the tops of your thighs. You bought it when you were with me because I persuaded you that it was the exact color of your eyes and perfect for a seduction scene if you ever let your guard down enough to seduce someone. So he was probably even more intrigued when he saw you in it. He was probably hoping you would climb him like a tree after he saw you in it."

"I'm not going to seduce him."

"You say that now. I'm an objective third party and I can tell you it was like watching the banter between Batman and Catwoman. You'll either seduce him, or you'll let him seduce you. Probably after you try to throw each other down or you try to scratch him with your imaginary claws. But no matter what happens, at least I can say I made sure you had a bathrobe appropriate for said seduction."

"Not going to happen," I firmly reiterate.

"Keep telling yourself that, Fierce Girl," she mimics his use of my nickname down to the sexy way he draws out each syllable.

"Ugh. Go away," I ineffectually attempt to shoo her away before I smack her for her impertinence like some irritable dowager aunt.

She laughs huskily. "I'm going away. I'm going away to start a betting pool. And this time I intend to win, unlike my bet about Taren and Zane."

I should've known she was too observant to miss the sparks between me and the town's newest villain turned savior.

Chapter 11

Blake

I'm certain that she's comparing herself to that lady's companion in the book she's reading. To me, she's not someone who will ever blend into the background. She captivates my attention no matter where she's standing in a room – whether it's the center of the ballroom or a dark, dusty alcove. She's always at the forefront of my thoughts while I try to figure out how to make her see who I truly am and at the same time ensure my coaching and teaching make a difference.

I've gotten to know my team over the last couple of weeks and their hesitant hopefulness has me feeling optimistic about our first official game of the season. We won two of our three pre-season skirmishes, but it's time to see whether the training paid off. The girls' team played first and won handily. I'm giving a pep talk when the opposing coach motions me over.

"What's up?" I ask, irritated at the interruption.

"We don't have a referee," he grimly informs me.

"What happened?" I don't want to reschedule or forfeit. My team has worked too hard for this and has been looking forward to it too much over the last three weeks.

"He has food poisoning or something. Do you know anyone that can sub? Like immediately?" He sounds as desperate as I suddenly feel.

"I'm relatively new in town, so no," I wish Zane wasn't out of town. I know he'd step in. But he and Taren are talking to a distributor on the east coast.

"I can ref for you," her voice is unmistakable, and her offer is unexpected. Since when would she volunteer to save my ass? She's kept her distance since the kiss that turned to breathless groping against her door. Like she really does think I'm kryptonite and being anywhere near me will be her ultimate downfall.

I turn around to face her. "Don't you have some celebrating to do? It's the first game of the season and you've already started your winning streak."

"It can wait. You're not going to be able to find someone on such short notice. And I know you'd do the same for me," she guilelessly confirms.

"You're sure you don't mind?" I would do the same for her. Even if she's determined to treat me like a bug on her windshield.

"No, Coach Armitage, I don't mind," I know the formality is for the benefit of the visiting coach.

I turn back to him. "Is that okay with you?"

"Yeah. Anything to stop us from cancelling the game."

Now I'm confident we're going to win. We've been practicing hard, and the referee is going to make all the calls in our favor.

An hour later, I'm fuming. I haven't agreed with more than half of her calls. She seems determined to show preference to the visiting team. I can't tell whether the calls are because of spite or because she doesn't want to be accused of favoring her home team. I'm banking on the latter rather than the former. I haven't given her a reason to act out of spite, and even though I throw her off her guard, she doesn't seem to resent me for it.

When one of my players makes a slide tackle in the box, she blows the whistle and calls foul. We're tied 3-3 and there is less than a minute left in the game. If she lets them have a penalty kick she's ensuring our loss. Suddenly I don't care who she is or how much I want to kiss her. She's trying to prove a point. She's trying to cement her impartiality and jacking up our chance to win in the process.

I'm crowding her, way up in her face. I don't want to be intimidating, but I'm barely keeping my temper in check. I can understand her need to appear impartial, but it's like she's deliberately sabotaging us. "What the hell are you doing? You just made sure we're going to lose."

She doesn't back down. Her brows are lowered, and her eyes are nothing but hard, inscrutable glitter, pinning me in place. "You're yellow carded. Step back," she commands. And then she has the audacity to blow her whistle in my face. She's formidable and antagonistic and I want to throw her over my shoulder and stride off the field. So I can kiss her senseless and spank that delicious peachy ass.

The shrill sound is still ringing in my ears as I stare at her in disbelief. "You're kicking me off the field?"

She nods affirmatively. She has a white-knuckled grip on the whistle. "You really feel threatened by me?" I'm angry and baffled. I want to kiss her more than ever. And tell her she's being contrary for no reason. This isn't some scene out of the Taming of the Shrew. Her stubbornness is costing us the game. My hands itch to glide over the curve of her ass and smack it.

"You're out of line. Get away from me and off the field."

"I'll get off your damn field, Fierce Girl," I rumble in warning. "But I don't go down without a fight and you just declared war."

I'm still in shock when I stride out of the locker room. I can't believe she blew that fucking whistle at me. I can't believe she carded me and kicked me out of the game. Like I'm an out-of-line belligerent teen. The guys took the results better than I expected. They said shit happens and a tie is still better than a loss. The other team missed their penalty kick. I still feel betrayed. Like she put a target on my back and did everything she could to hit it.

When I round the corner, she's walking toward me, sliding her phone into her pocket. I stop right in front of her and brace my hands against my hips. "What was that?" I bark.

"I was just doing my job. I had to show I was impartial," she affirms. "It was obvious I was stepping in as a favor to you, and I needed to make sure I didn't show prejudice against the visiting team."

"That didn't mean you had to sabotage us," I counter. "Every call that could've gone either way resulted in you giving the visiting team the advantage and throwing us under the bus," I don't even try to disguise my anger at her betrayal.

"Don't blame your team's inability to follow the rules on me," she fires back, her hands on her hips.

"You are so infuriating," I growl at her. I prowl toward her, and she warily steps backward, until she can't go any further because of the wall of lockers at her back. I pin her wrists in one hand and press her harder against the cold metal behind her.

"So are you," she growls right back.

"Right now I want to kiss you almost as much as I want to spank you."

She hisses in outrage. "In your dreams."

"Yes. You are. No matter how many times I take my cock in my own hand. I can't banish the image of you taking it in your hand instead, or the one of you kneeling in front of me as it hits the back of your throat. Or what it would feel like to sink into you from behind, with you bared to me on all fours, wet and begging for it," I confess.

She gasps. And her eyes darken.

The energy between us changes. It still has the burn of rage, but now it's morphing into something else. We're both shiny with sweat. I can smell the sharp tang of it rising in the air. The sudden arousal that's sparking along my spine feels ruthless and undeniable. It's an inexorable hurricane of want expanding between us. I know there's nothing on this earth that can tamp it down for me. I'm too caught up. Every curve and muscle of her insanely lithe body rests against mine and I feel her imprint more acutely than the drip of perspiration down the back of my neck or the anger that left the mark of my nails on my palms.

The infernal whistle that's the root of my anger rests in the hollow of her cleavage. I wrap my hand around it and press my knuckles against the sides of her breasts. Her lips thin to a mutinous line in the sand.

"What are you doing?" She hisses.

"I'm going to disrupt your train of thought like you're constantly disrupting mine," I slide my nose down the side of her throat, inhaling the scent of salt-damp skin seeping through the cotton of the tank. We're exchanging glares dark enough to pulverize each other's bones to dust. Like gladiators ready to grapple each other with our bare hands. Our breath mingles. Neither one of us is giving an inch.

"I dare you," she challenges. Her eyes are flinty and hard, her jaw clenched.

"You don't know what you've unleashed, Fierce Girl," I bend my head toward her, ignoring her upturned face. Instead, I drop my nose to the upper curve of her ear, then skim it to smell the subtle musk oozing from her pores in the little space behind her earlobe. My hand splays out, completely canvassing her now. I can feel her nipples harden beneath my palm, and I groan. She might want to eviscerate me, but she wants other things too. I have to use my touch to convince her I'm not her mortal enemy.

I slide my hand beneath her tank, and trail it along smooth skin that warms even more beneath my touch. I drag the elastic of her sports bra up, until the band is just below her neck. I hold it there in my fist while I look at her. Her breasts will overflow my hands. She has a cross dangling from one of her puffy, perfect nipples. I can't stop myself from bending down to skim my lips over it, taking it between my teeth and tugging gently. She moans and restlessly shifts her legs against mine.

I lick across her other nipple, sucking it into my mouth and swirling my tongue around it until it's a hardened pebble I want to lave until she squirms. Her head and shoulders are thrown back against the wall of lockers, but the lower half of her body is grinding against me like she's going to swallow me whole. I lift her leg and wrap it around my waist so I can wedge myself in the cradle of her thighs. The thin barrier of her yoga pants isn't doing anything to disguise how wet and swollen my mouth and hands are making her, and I'm ready to poke through my shorts. I bend my knees and swoop up, so I slide right against her. She bears down on me, her arms shaking around my neck.

I nuzzle her ear again, and I'm about to steal another kiss when she puts both hands on my chest and pushes me away. "No. I don't want this," she says shakily and yanks down her bra and shirt.

Even though she made me so angry I could spit nails, I would never force a woman. I step away. I can't make her want this, want me. My anger has completely evaporated. Now I just want to claim her. And grinding against her in a deserted school hallway isn't the way to convince her. I want to explore her in excruciating detail, learn the source of every moan and whimper and sigh. Until she thinks of my hands as her own. Until she wants to claim them for herself.

I shouldn't be shocked at how quickly things escalated. I can still taste the bite of cold metal against the roof of my mouth. I want to map her body with my callouses, find out if she has any more piercings. Or tattoos. I hope she has tattoos. Maybe we can play a game of you show me yours and I'll show you mine. Her body is a treasure map I can't wait to explore. I want to see her hair pouring over my hands, her back arching when my teeth graze the tips of her breasts again.

And I want to explore her now. But I'm going to wait for her to come to me. If it's her decision, even if she regrets it, she'll have to own it. I already know she's going to ruin me for all other partners.

"You know where to find me if you change your mind." I salute her and lope away. I resist looking over my shoulder because I can feel that death stare stabbing me in the back. I'm no longer mad because I get that every move she makes is meant to distract me from chasing her.

The potential of what we could build, what we could become, is enough to incinerate every last particle of my anger. She wouldn't be trying so hard to prove she's unaffected or trying to come across as the most neutral referee ever if she wasn't finding it hard to be objective.

Chapter 12

Sarah

It's been two weeks since his mouth made a carnal acquaintance with my body. It's mid-October and Taren and Zane invited us all to a masquerade party. I was going to refuse because I knew he'd be there, and Taren told me she would make sure I was eating Thanksgiving dinner at the Chinese takeout place if I didn't show. So of course I caved. Zane has serious skills in the kitchen and Emma is making the desserts.

I've been freezing him out at every opportunity. If he comes into a room, I either exit immediately, or, if that's not possible, steadfastly ignore him. He's not acting at all like I expected him to. Instead of chasing the next glittery shiny thing, his eyes follow my every move. The breakroom chatter has been disgruntled. All the single teachers have him in their sights and he's yet to accept any of their blatant invitations. He barely acknowledges them. He's polite but oblivious to their come-ons. He hasn't approached me. He's waiting for me to make the first move or give a not-so-subtle hint that it's okay for him to make it.

We've just started our segment on Oceanography in my AP biology class when someone knocks impatiently on the door. Of course he's standing there. "What do you want?"

He raises a brow. "Still hostile, I see," he brushes past me, and I close my eyes in exasperation. "I'm here to observe because now apparently I'll be teaching an AP class as well."

"You're here to observe on whose suggestion?" I suspiciously ask. I think it's just an excuse to get in my space because I've been ignoring him. He's like a persistent gnat.

Because we live in the greater Chesapeake Bay watershed, we're talking about the Eastern Oyster. It has some intriguing evolution, and I don't relish his peanut gallery ribald commentary when I talk about it. I already expect guffaws and tasteless jokes from the two lacrosse players.

"I'm here at the suggestion of Principal Greene. According to him, your students consistently score fours and fives on the exam. He wants me to observe and learn."

"Fine," I grumble. "But no off-the-cuff inappropriate comments."

"Scouts' honor," he assures me.

I respond to his promise with a very exaggerated eye roll because I seriously doubt he was ever a scout. "Whatever. Find somewhere to sit and don't interrupt."

"Mmmm...bossy," he mutters under his breath. "I like it."

He's so obnoxious. I'd like to show him bossy. He already made it a point to talk about rulers.

"So, can anyone tell me what is so unique about the reproductive cycle of the Virginia Oyster?"

Madison Griffin's hand immediately shoots into the air. I nod my head for her to proceed.

"They change sex. They're male and become female at one year."

"Yes, that's correct, Madison," I turn to address the entire class. "Can anyone tell me why this has been crucial to the survival of the species?"

Madison's hand shoots up again. I know she's the valedictorian and a voracious reader, but I want some of the other students to show me they've also done the reading. "Anyone else?" I give the lacrosse players reclining in the corner a pointed look. They don't acknowledge it because their attention is completely absorbed by their phones.

Blake raises his hand. "You are not a student."

"And if I know the answer? Won't it save you time?"

"Yes, but again, you're not a student," I reiterate.

"Maybe I'm setting a good example for those two gentlemen over there," he gestures toward the inattentive lacrosse players. He twists around in his chair. "Gentlemen," he snaps. They finally lift their heads from their phones.

"Yes, Coach Armitage?" The center, Alex Graham, asks.

"Have you been paying attention to Ms. Fraser?"

He gives me a sheepish look. "No," he mumbles.

"Well you need to change that. Because no matter how well you play lacrosse, you still need to make it through college with a degree you can use. She's trying to make sure you're ready for that. Stop wasting her time and pay attention. Answer her question since she won't let me answer it, Mr. Graham."

Alex swallows. "Ms. Fraser, can you please repeat the question?"

"Yes, Alex. I would like for you to tell me why the unique reproductive cycle of the Virginia Oyster has been essential to its survival."

His brow crinkles. "Wait a second, don't they like change sexes?"

I nod my head and tap my foot impatiently.

"So, that means they don't need both genders to survive. That they have a greater chance of survival because they're both genders," he concludes.

"Although you've used circular reasoning, Mr. Graham, that is a correct analysis. Good job."

Blake is quiet for the duration of the class. When the bell rings, he gives me a nod of respect. "Ms. Fraser, I understand why your students have some of the highest passing scores in the state. You manage to make science more interesting than I ever thought it could be," he reaches his hand out to shake mine. I offer it and he just clasps it, running his fingers over my knuckles. "I thought you might want to know that I'll be joining you at the book club meeting later this week," he leans forward to whisper in my ear. He hovers there, his breath stirring the tendrils of hair that escaped from my braid.

"Why? Do you think reading those books will give you some sort of insight about me?" I'm scared to hear his answer.

He just shakes his head back and forth, like he's chiding me for being an errant child.

I'm about to yank my hand away when he drops it like a hot potato. He gives a little bow in my direction and turns on his heel. He doesn't look back when he walks away. I wonder if he knows I'm watching him.

I'm dressed like a martial version of Little Red Riding Hood. There's a basket full of homemade brownies on my arm and I paired my red cape with a full-length body suit and my black combat boots. I think I look I could kick someone's ass or seduce them into doing anything I want. Exactly the combination I was going for.

I see him lounging against the fence with Zane, Dex, Ian and a couple of other guys I don't recognize. His eyes light on me immediately and I can feel them burning a hole between my shoulder blades, but I ignore him.

Taren grabs my hand and pulls me toward the table laden with food. There's a crystal punch bowl sitting in the middle full of orange liquid. Knowing Zane, I'm sure it's spiked with something guaranteed to make me forget my own name. I grab a plastic cup and fill it to the brim. "We haven't talked all week," she crosses her arms over her chest and impatiently taps her foot.

I shrug. "I've been busy." It's not an excuse or an exaggeration. I *have* been busy. But I've also been avoiding her, and she knows it.

She narrows her eyes. "You just don't want me meddling."

"It's not that," I half-heartedly protest.

"Then what exactly is it?" She raises a brow and I know she won't let this go.

"Yeah, what is it?" Emma breaks in with her rich contralto as she saunters over. She's dressed like a sex kitten version of Elphaba.

"It's that there's nothing to tell."

"I don't believe you. Zane told me Blake was amazingly calm after the soccer game, even though he looked livid when you carded him."

"There's no way he calmed down that fast without some incentive or sexy mojo," chimes in Emma.

"And Zane said he saw him stomp into the school hot on your heels."

"We had a confrontation," I concede.

Emma gleefully rubs her hands together. "Please tell me it ended in a hate fuck."

She's so demented. "You've been reading too many mafia romances," I tell her. "No, it didn't quite end in a hate fuck."

"So there was fucking? Or hating?" she eagerly asks.

"There was hate," I admit. "But it fizzled out pretty quickly when he caged me against the lockers."

"You almost had locker sex?" breathes Emma. "That's so kinky and hot."

"Well it kind of fits tonight's theme," Taren excitedly interjects.

Emma and I groan in unison.

"What do you guys have planned?"

"We paired everyone with a partner for the games."

"And let me guess... Blake is my partner?"

"Well, duh. You guys get to bob for apples, and team up for Horror Movie Trivia and Spooky Charades."

That doesn't sound too onerous. "Those don't sound so bad."

"Speak for yourself," grumbles Emma.

"Weren't you saying you needed something to take your mind off work? You're consumed by your bakery. Three quarters of our friend nights are just so we can taste test your new recipes. You need to make time to play. Zane said a couple of the firemen are intrigued by you."

"I don't need any distractions. I'm like Emma – I want flings from out of town so they don't interfere."

Taren just shakes her head at the two of us. "I'm telling both of you that you don't know what you're missing. It's really nice to sleep beside someone who gets you."

"I don't suppose Zane is making the same argument?" I ask.

"Of course he is. He wants all of his friends to find happiness. He worries about them," her eyes slide to Dex. "Especially the town mechanic."

"Did you invite Marianela?" whispers Emma.

"I did, but she's on shift. I paired him with the vet assistant."

We all silently wonder how that will go. Dex is an inscrutable man of very few words. He thinks his scars are a turn-off, but they're exactly the opposite. If he bothered to crook his little finger he'd easily have a revolving door of women more than willing to heal him.

Zane interrupts the hubbub of conversation, clapping his hands together. "We're gonna eat and then play games.

Here's who's paired with who." He reads the couples from a piece of crumpled paper he pulls out of his pocket.

Blake strides toward me, grinning from ear to ear.

"Don't look so excited," I demand.

"I can't help it. Horror movies are my jam – we're going to kill the competition."

"Is that supposed to be a play on words?"

"Maybe. I mean we do have cornfields all around us we could hide the bodies in."

I laugh at his exaggerated grimace. "This is not *Children of the Corn*."

"Well it could be. Or it could be *The Wicker Man*. I mean Emma is dressed like a very convincing witch. I can see her sacrificing clueless guys."

"But I think Taren's supposed to be Tinkerbell to Zane's Captain Hook. That doesn't broadcast human sacrifice."

He snorts. "No, it broadcasts their tendency to role play."

"Did all of you dress like pirates on purpose?"

He's wearing an eyepatch, he has a stuffed parrot on his shoulder, and his billowing white shirt is open to his navel, where it's tucked into a pair of tight leather pants. I can easily picture him gracing the front of a clinch cover.

"We did. We thought it would be funny, and the costume was easy to pull together." His eyes roam over me. "You're the sexiest Little Red Riding Hood I've ever seen," he gutturally informs me.

"I was going for kick-ass vibes too."

"I'm getting those too," he confirms, his eyes growing even darker.

He wasn't lying about his trivia knowledge. He even knew the obscure ones. The winning question was to name Carrie White's mom. He nailed it, and even talked about her weird prayer closet. We didn't win the charades game though, that was all Emma and one of the firemen. So all that's left now is bobbing for apples. Taren assured us she left plenty of the stems intact.

I'm first. I'm bent over the trough, and I know Blake's gaze is glued to my butt while he holds my cape out of the way. I'm chasing the one with the longest stem when something bumps against us from behind. I end up half in the trough, soaking wet. But that makes it easier to grasp the apple.

Blake pulls me close to steady me.

When I twist around, I see Emma galloping across the yard, the fireman in hot pursuit. I shake my head at her antics.

"You got the apple," Blake brushes aside the dripping hanks of my hair.

"I did," I agree. "I hope we win. Despite what Taren said, she didn't make it easy."

"Well half of the guests already bowed out because they said it was gross and unhygienic," he shrugs. "Our only competition was Emma and I think she's otherwise occupied."

We're declared the winners of the night's festivities. "So what's the prize?" asks Blake.

"It's something Sarah's been craving," Taren smiles as she hands me a gift card to Dairy Queen. "She has an affinity for ice cream and now you'll be forced to witness it."

"Yes!" I shout and triumphantly thrust my fist in the air.

"So when should we sample what they have on offer?" Blake asks suggestively.

He looks like he's proposing a frolic, not just an ice cream date. "How about we go after the next game?" It's more than a week away and that'll give me plenty of time to mentally prepare myself for the experience. This sounds like an actual date, unlike the drinks and darts we shared weeks ago.

"Sounds good," he casually agrees. "Are you going to be at bookclub tomorrow night?" he adroitly changes the subject.

"I plan to be. Are you going to be there?" I ask curiously.

"Yep. I finished last night."

So apparently Zane really did convert him. Or he meant what he said about using romance books to learn new seduction techniques.

His head is thrown back in laughter, his Adam's apple bobbing in the curve of his sleek muscled throat. He has his arms slung across the back of the chair and he's straddling it. His eyes flash to mine when I stop at the edge of the circle of chairs. Of course the only empty one is the one beside him. Taren and Emma are on the other side of Zane and Dex isn't here tonight. This sword dance between us is exhausting and I'm going to do my best to ignore him. He has me hovering over a wall of burning flame, suspended above the parachute stretched out to catch me that's ten stories down. His gambit in my classroom earlier this week, and the forced partnership at the Halloween party, have made me even more determined to act like he doesn't even exist.

"I told you I'd be here," he smugly informs me once I'm sitting there with my legs crossed at the ankles, my book in my lap and my attention focused on Ms. Bromwell.

"I still don't know why you bothered," I murmur darkly.

"According to Zane, reading these books is the way to unlock the secrets women keep. A much better approach than dissecting that Mel Gibson movie."

I snort. I can't help myself. "*What Women Want*? Yeah, fooling a woman into believing you understand her in order to steal her job isn't a good idea."

"Well it's not the technique I intend to use on you."

"None of your techniques will work on me."

"Not even befriending your overprotective dog or giving you the one thing you've been coveting but think you don't deserve?"

"Not even that. One, you'll never gain Sasha's loyalty. And two, there's no way you'll ever be able to figure out what I want and what I need."

"Hey, you two. Stop glowering at each other," Zane snaps his fingers at us in reprimand. "If that's what you call flirting you both seriously need to pay attention to this discussion."

Taren thumps him on the shoulder and mimes zipping her mouth. He grins and shakes his head. "Nope," he replies and leans forward to nuzzle her cheek.

Fuck my life if Zane's determined to matchmake Blake and me. I've learned he can be ruthless when he has a goal he wants to achieve, and our protests are just going to make him even more committed to getting the result he wants. Hopefully, Taren will talk some sense into him. I doubt it, though. She seemed to be on the Blake train as well at our dinner a couple of weeks ago.

All the whispering stops abruptly when the librarian claps her hands together. "Before we begin, I want to welcome the newest member of the Willow Creek Wantons, Blake Armitage. Blake read tonight's book but is catching up on the rest of the series. He's new to the romance genre, so let's go easy on him."

There are a couple of nods and a few polite claps.

"Not to put our newest member on the spot, but is there anything that stood out to you about this month's book, Mr. Armitage?" She looks at Blake expectantly, like pearls of wisdom are going to fall out of his mouth.

I know he listened to the audiobook and I'm curious as to what resonated with him the most.

He clears his throat nervously and I almost feel sorry for him.

"Well, Phoebe is the kind of woman who thinks she's unnoticeable and inobtrusive. But she's not, she never has been. Her sparkle is like moonbeams, more gentle and subtle than the glaring sunlight, because she doesn't flaunt it. But it's captivating all the same. Dryden's an idiot for ever believing he could relegate her to a single corner of his life as only a mistress. It's obvious she completes him because she understands him like no one ever has and sees what he's really like under the polished image that fools everyone else. He should've just offered her marriage instead of hurting her feelings like that," he concludes somewhat defiantly. "That's probably why I appreciated Dryden's sacrifice so much. It's obvious that he isn't fond of Charybdis. But he still rescues him because he's important to someone he loves and he's making a grand gesture to show that person how he feels."

I'm stunned. When he told me he was attending the discussion, I assumed he just skimmed it. He didn't. He read it and his observations are insightful and thought provoking. He's very passionate about the story. The room is quiet, and I think we're all bowled over.

"Thank you for your insight, Mr. Armitage. I completely agree," Ms. Bromwell reels us all back in. "Does anyone have thoughts on why Phoebe seems to underestimate her appeal? Is it tied to her situation or something deeper?"

This time it's Zane who jumps in and soon there's a lively debate about how tainted our self-perception can be in relation to those around us.

Chapter 13

Sarah

I WANT TO TEST this hypothesis I saw on TikTok that said wine goblets were designed to hold an entire bottle of wine. And not think about my man-bunned, leatherjacket wearing, tattooed neighbor who is now a romance reader and a Pennyroyal Green convert.

The wind is wailing like a crazed banshee, beating its chest, and thumping its head against the walls in honor of a fallen hero's Irish wake. The rain is lashing the double-paned windows like an army on the march, a steady cadence. I'm huddling in my shabby, velvet-nubbed armchair, with Sasha's head nestled in my lap. It's one of my favorite thrift store finds, and I like to curl up in it and read. Rainstorms have an inherent loneliness that forces me to contemplate the choices that led me to Willow Creek. And I don't like the contemplation of sitting still and staring out the window because it forces too many memories to the surface. Too many things better left in the past, lying sedated instead of caterwauling at the edges of my consciousness for acknowledgement. Losing myself in a historical romance is my favorite form of escapism. One of my bookish besties swears that the eighth book, *It Happened One Midnight*, is her fave in the whole series, and I'm excited to see what the hype is all about. Supposedly the hero Jonathan is the reigning darts king of Pennyroyal Green. I wonder if Blake will feel an affinity with him.

My wine glass is empty, but I lick the drops from the rim. The last sip trickles down my throat, bittersweet. I run my fingers along my Sasha's scruffy neck, scratching behind her silky ears as she burrows her head into my touch. She whines softly, and it echoes in the quiet of the room, breaking it apart like a motorboat does the solitude of the lake at dawn.

I still don't know why I let him maul me against the lockers last week. My composure was in pieces afterward. I don't let people get under my skin like that. I can't. The fear that they will expect me to give more than I'm capable of giving, to make token appearances and meet big, gregarious families and friend groups keeps me from opening up. I'm always afraid that I won't be enough.

I still think he's arrogant and entitled and used to always getting what he wants. I don't need the complications he would bring to a life I am content with. A part of me longs for the connection I see between Taren and Zane, and I'm definitely, ashamedly envious of what they share. But I'm convinced a bond like theirs isn't something Blake Armitage can offer anyone. He's a taker. I've been around them for most of my life, and I can identify them at first sight. I know if I succumb to the temptation of those lips, I'll be taken.

I wake up disoriented because a splash of cold water hits me directly in the face and Sash is whimpering and cringing beside me. Her entire body is shaking. As I rub the grit from my eyes, I realize I can see the moon behind the clouds because half of the cabin roof is gone. It's been completely ripped away, and there's a huge tree trunk lying less than twenty feet away. It barely missed us.

It's still storming outside. I can feel the house shake every time there's a boom of thunder, and I know I need to get us out as soon as possible before the walls collapse around us. I'm gingerly crawling through the splintered furniture and shards of glass when I hear someone yelling my name at the top of their lungs.

"Here!" I croak out.

"Sarah, where are you?" Someone bellows. I can hear the desperation and fear in their voice.

"Here, I'm here!" I manage to yell a little louder. And then he's there, sweeping me into his arms. I feel his lips brush my forehead and it's surreal. Blake Armitage being tender? With anyone?

"Please tell me you're ok," he reels back, clasping my chin between his thumb and forefinger. Even in the dim light I can see his panicked expression.

I tentatively shake my head. "Nothing broken," I croak. "It just missed us." About six hours ago, I was telling myself what a bad decision he would be. So why am I relishing his touch? Why do I have the urge to burrow closer?

"I spent a summer timbering out west and knew the sound as soon as I heard it. I got here as fast as I could.

Thank God you're safe," he sweeps me into his arms and snaps his fingers for Sash to follow. She wrinkles her nose at him, and I'm amazed when she immediately falls behind us.

He picks his way across the minefield of debris like an expert. I should be protesting, but I'm in shock. "Where are you taking me?"

"Next door," he answers, with a brief glance down. He doesn't even break his stride.

"Your place?" I can hear how shaky my voice is, and I tell myself it's only because of the shock, not because I'm thinking of the kiss again that veered into dangerous territory. Or how I'm being reminded of my reasons for avoiding him.

"Yes, I'm the closest," he peers down at me again. "I promise I'm not going to ravage you or take advantage."

"That's not what I'm worried about," I mutter under my breath. I'm more concerned that I'll ravage him. Especially when I'm feeling so raw and vulnerable. It's how I've used sex in the past – to silence my demons.

"Well, whatever it is you're worried about, don't. You can stay at my place for as long as you need to. It can be completely platonic, no pressure," he reassures me as he jogs up his steps.

He settles me on an overstuffed couch and motions Sasha over. She nudges my hand, making sure I'm ok. She can sense how anxious I am, and it's affecting her. Even though she followed us into the house when Blake asked her to, she still lays her ears back when she looks up at him. It's a warning that she'll protect me if she needs to. It's a warning that she's tolerating him but won't be rolling over for belly rubs any time soon.

"She's very protective," he observes.

"Yes. I've had her since she was a puppy," what I don't say is that she's my best friend and has been the most dependable part of my life since I adopted her from a rescue organization seven years ago. We made the cross-country trip to Willow Creek together, and she will always be my ride or die.

He reaches out a hand to stroke her head and she growls. He snatches it back. "Ok. So not ready to be friends yet. I'm still glad you're here to help take care of her," his voice is low and soothing, and her ears prick forward.

Of course he has dog whisperer skills on top of everything else.

He turns toward me again. "I bought some chamomile tea at the farmer's market. Would you like some?"

I nod yes and squelch myself further into my perch on his couch.

"Okay. Let me grab a blanket and then I'll put the kettle on," he disappears for a second. When he comes back, he's carrying a blanket. "It's weighted, I hope that doesn't bother you."

"That's what I have too," after a long day of dealing with overstimulation, nothing calms me faster than sitting on my couch with hot tea and my blanket.

"I have some I made that aren't, but I thought you might need it right now," he kneels before me and nudges me forward. His lips rest against my forehead while he wraps the blanket around me. Once he tucks the end snugly in, he slides a knuckle along the upper curve of my cheek. "You don't know how glad I am that you're safe," he doesn't have that panicked look anymore, but he still seems shaken.

The beginning of his admission dawns on me. "Some that you made?"

He gives me a bashful grin and rakes his hand through his hair. "I like to crochet in the evenings. It helps quiet my ADHD and keeps my hands busy while I'm binge watching."

"I never would've expected that from you," I confess. It's a hobby I never would have guessed. I wonder how many other people know that about him. Am I one of a privileged few or does he hand out knitted caps and lap covers to everyone at Christmas? Just thinking about that big hand wielding a crochet needle makes me want to know more. Makes me want to kiss him again. It's a little nerdy, a lot appealing. "I knew you'd be full of surprises. That's probably why I've been so determined to keep my distance."

"Even though you've been aloof, it's been impossible to abandon the hope that I can change your mind," he replies.

"I've never thought of us as enemies, but you throw my world off its axis, and I don't think I'm ready for that."

"We're not enemies. At least I don't think we're, and I don't want us to be. Even though you drive me crazy, I'll settle for being your friend. I can wait until you're ready for me to be more. Because, despite what you believe, Sarah Fraser, I'm in Willow Creek to stay."

With that enigmatic comment, he straightens up and heads toward what I assume is the kitchen. I'm pondering what he meant when he said I drive him crazy, and then my eyes flutter shut.

I wake up disoriented again. There's a hand clasped around my waist and a solid leg between mine. My cheek is nestled against a bicep, and I hear Sasha's soft little snuffles as she snores away on the floor beside us. I can't believe I didn't stir when he arranged us on the couch. I don't cuddle. And that's exactly what we're doing. Strangely, I have no desire to extricate myself from the warm cocoon of his body. I feel the safest and calmest I've felt in a long time. I hope it isn't all due to him.

Every time I let people in and give them the power to allay my fears it ends in disaster.

Chapter 14

Blake

I CAN'T BELIEVE SHE'S in my house, on my couch, in my arms. She ties me up in knots. But it feels so right to have her lying beside me. Even if I have a crick in my neck from the weird angle and my arm is tingling because it fell asleep under her head. I ease up and nuzzle the crown of her loose ponytail. She smells like rainwater and sunshine.

She stirs and for a second I think she's waking up. She just burrows deeper against my neck. I very slowly remove myself from her embrace and replace my arms with the pillow. She breathes a deep sigh and buries her nose in it.

I stand there for what feels like hours. Just staring down at her contented profile. Her ponytail is half undone, and her hair trails down her back in a shimmering waterfall, almost to her waist. I reach down, sliding my fingers through it.

I know I need to call Dex and let him know about the damage. I reluctantly leave her side and head out to the deck. The sky is clear and blue, and you'd never know that Mother Nature wreaked complete and utter havoc last night.

He answers on the first ring. "You have bad news. Because you never call me this early."

He sounds resigned. "Yeah, it's pretty bad, but I think I can handle it for now." I fill him in on the storm damage and let him know that I'm heading into town to buy a tarp to protect her place until we can get it under a new roof.

"I'm sending over a buddy of mine that's an arborist to remove the tree. But he probably won't be able to make it until tomorrow," he pauses, like he's weighing his next words. "I know you can't stop thinking about her, but will shacking up cloud your decision-making skills?"

It's a fair question, but I think I'm already too captivated to care what happens. "I don't think so. She's pretty much under my skin to stay and being this close to her can't make things worse."

"Keep telling yourself that," he grumbles. "But if you're okay with it, that works for me. At least I won't have to foot an additional lodging bill and make the repairs too," he pauses. "You know Zane is going to be annoying about this, right? You'll be the perfect guinea pig for his forced proximity theory."

"Well, I'm kind of hoping I prove his theory, so I'll tolerate his jibes." And I'm going to snag her library book and read it. It obviously contains successful wooing tactics and I need all the help I can get.

"There will be a lot of jibes and jabs. He's going to find this whole situation intriguing and he's not going to let it rest. Better you than me. Maybe if he's hyper-focused on you he'll stop giving me shit about Marianela."

I can hear his grimace through the phone. "Someday I need to hear that story."

"It's not pretty. We had our moment and it passed. But yeah, some day when I'm wallowing in self-pity I'll share all the gory details."

"I'm thinking about grilling out tonight to take her mind off things, do you want to come over? I'm inviting Zane too."

"I need that tonight. I have a feeling today is going to be a shit day because I'm the only autobody shop in town. I'll show up around seven with beer in hand."

I wake up for the second time, disoriented. I'm lying on the couch by myself, and Sasha's on the other side of the room. She's crouched down, completely entranced by whatever she found in the corner. I wrap the blanket around me and skid toward her in my socks. She has her nose within inches of a little round ball of spotted fur. Whatever it is, it's curled up defensively. I'm guessing it's his notorious guinea pig. It has a tiny purple bow tie on, and the spots look familiar, like the cute creature he had cuddled in his lap in his Instagram stories last week.

"Sasha, no!" I scold. I snap my fingers. "Heel." She wags her tail at the guinea pig and wriggles in excitement before she reluctantly sidles up to me. I'm petting her when I hear the thump of boots landing in the foyer. A moment later, Blake walks toward us.

"I was going to wake you if you weren't up yet. I invited our friends over for a barbecue to take your mind off things."

As soon as I took my hand off Sasha's ruff, she crept toward the ball of fur again. Blake watches the exchange, smiling crookedly at the stand-off. "I think she may have found your pet guinea pig. She's completely enthralled," I explain with embarrassment.

He glances over to the corner. "Yep. She found Woodrow Wilson. My pet guinea pig and my new sidekick."

"So he's not just your pet – he's your sidekick. That's kind of adorable. You're just full of surprises," I can't control my gushing admiration. He doesn't seem like the kind of guy who cuddles guinea pigs, and it makes him even more appealing.

Like he's just been digging around in my head, he bends over and scoops Woodrow Wilson into his arms. "Hey little buddy," he murmurs and strokes its head.

My ovaries just exploded.

"I know I don't seem like the kind of guy who would have a pet guinea pig. It doesn't exactly go with the motorcycle or the tattoos or what you call my playboy persona."

He smiles to himself. "But my little sister Ellery convinced me to get him, and she's already excited about ordering every weird costume for him she can find," he shakes his head in amusement.

"He's probably going to be the main focus of your Instagram stories..."

He chuckles. "Yeah, Ellery suggested that too. She said it makes me more approachable."

"Well, if your number of followers is any indication, I'd say she's right." It could also be because it's not just my ovaries over here exploding, but I don't say that. Pretty sure he doesn't need me expanding his ego. I decide it's time to change the subject before I inadvertently give myself away. "You said you're hosting a barbecue tonight?" I hope he can't hear the anxiety in my voice. "Is there anything I need to do?" I don't think I'm ready to face anyone yet. I'm still reeling from the disaster, still trying to process what it means and what I need to do and worried about what my renter's insurance is going to cover. It'd be just my luck that they have some stupid act of God clause that bars me from getting compensation for anything that was ruined. Just contemplating it gives me a headache and I reach up to rub my temples.

"You don't need to do anything. You have enough to worry about already. I thought you'd like the distraction, and the alcohol. I'm going to make white sangria for you, Taren and Emma and the Dex and Zane are bringing beer. I prepped the potato salad while you were still asleep and the ground beef for the burgers is thawing out in the fridge." He moves toward me, and removes my hands from my temples, replacing them with his own. I sink gratefully into his touch. He's kneading right where I need it. He presses a kiss to my forehead. "I told you I would take care of you."

"I don't want to be a burden." I feel a little overwhelmed by how he seems to have thought of everything. It still turns me on though. I didn't even know I had a competency kink until now.

"Why don't you go take a shower?" He puts his hands on my shoulders. "I'll make us a snack to tide us over and we'll head over to your place to check things out in the light of day."

I shake my head in agreement, woozy from his attention. Still out of sorts and half awake.

I make myself snap out of it and shuffle toward the back of the house. The layout of his cabin is exactly like mine, and I know that's where I'll find the guest bathroom.

I don't know why I'm so nervous. It's only a small back-yard barbecue and everyone coming is in our mutual friend circle. But he rescued me, and now I'm staying in his house. Using his soap and his coffee mugs. Drinking chamomile tea and snuggling under him and his blankets. I still feel shaky and don't know if I can handle seeing how much of my life was destroyed by that freaking tree. I know I should just be grateful that I'm safe and sound. That he found me before I was hurt. But my cabin was the first place that was truly mine – a carefully curated sanctuary that made me feel like a warm hug whenever I stepped inside. I don't know what I'll be able to salvage, and I don't know if I'll be able to replace the special things I need to replace. I can feel my heart beating in my throat like the rushed staccato of hummingbird wings, and I brace my hands on the sink and hang my head to swallow down my riot of emotions.

"Sarah, are you okay? I wanted to take a quick shower too, but I don't want to disturb you," he sounds worried, and his voice jerks me back to reality.

"I'll be fine," I reassure him through the door.

"You don't sound fine," he replies. I can hear the worry again, and a teeny thread of frustration. "You can talk to me, Fierce Girl. I'm here to help."

"I'm not used to asking anyone for help." I'm not. I'm used to handling everything myself and telling everyone that I'm okay. Even when I'm not. Because I think that's what they want to hear.

"I'm the same way. It's hard to let other people in when you're so used to them letting you down. I don't know if that's what happened to you, but that's definitely the place I'm coming from," he sighs, and there's a gentle thump on the other side of the door. Instinctively, I know that was his forehead hitting the wood.

"It's hard for me to trust other people too. But I'm worried about other stuff," I admit.

"I know you're worried about your house. I already let Dex know the situation and it will be repaired as soon as possible. Meanwhile, I thought we could go over and assess the damage and do what we can to protect your belongings."

"That's exactly what I need. Thank you, Shark," I'm glad he can't see me, because there's a lump in my throat and my eyes are swimming with tears. I'm overwhelmed by his understanding. I splash my face with cold water and emerge from my cocoon, the anxiety held at bay for the moment.

He's leaning against one wall, his head bent over his phone, his thumb scrolling through what looks like text messages. "Hey, Fierce Girl."

His smile is like the gooey caramel center of one of my favorite Ghirardelli chocolates, softening the hard lines of his face, filled with a warm invitation and a depth of understanding I wouldn't have thought him capable of two weeks ago.

"Can we go over now?" I eagerly ask.

He grabs my clasped hands and brings them to his lips, planting soft kisses across the tops of my knuckles. I must have been twisting them in front of him. I try to pull away, embarrassed by my weakness. He gives me a chiding look. "No. I'm holding your hand because I think you're going to need it. And because I want to. I hope that answers your question."

"So we're going over there now?" I repeat. He shakes his head in confirmation. "Thank you."

"I know the suspense is eating you alive, and I can sense you chasing your worry around in an endless loop, like a cat chasing its tail. Let's do what we can to alleviate some of your anxiety."

He leads me outside. The sky is the deepest, clearest blue I've ever seen. Like it's professing its innocence and didn't rip my life apart a couple of days ago. I want to shake my fist at it. Or scream obscenities. Or both.

The tree is still there. The house looks eerily intact except for that one undeniable intrusion. "How bad do you think it is?" I know he can hear the tremor in my voice, but I'm helpless to hold it in.

"I think that the rain probably did more damage than the tree. It was a clean break."

I take a deep breath and push through the open door. His hand hovers at the small of my back as we cross the threshold, there in case I need it. In case I stumble. Or I suspect in case I break into uncontrollable sobbing. He's probably figured out by now that I don't let that happen where anyone else can see. The fact that he's offering comfort all the same is like a cloak of invincibility and gives me the courage to step forward. My eyes sweep through the room that received the lion's share of devastation. The recliner is toast. And so is the tv. But my books and my vintage records are intact. The roof is still offering a thin shelf of protection. I'm relieved that it isn't worse.

The recliner and the tv are easily replaced. My books and records wouldn't have been. The fact that I won't be able to live in my space for at least four weeks is daunting, but it's not the tragedy I was expecting.

"It was so scary when it was happening. I felt like Dorothy, like I was a teacup sloshing around in the middle of a tempest. But in the daylight, it's far better than I was expecting," I confide with relief.

"It's a lot better than I expected too. It's not supposed to rain again until next week, so the guys and I will put tarps up tomorrow to protect your books and records and move the couch into the alcove. Dex is having a crew come in tomorrow morning to cut the tree into logs and get it out of the way, so we should be able to protect everything tomorrow afternoon. Then we can tarp the roof as well."

"Do we have tarps?"

"Yeah, I went into town and got a couple, and Dex dropped off some huge ones this morning. They're in my garage. I'll go grab them so they're here when we need them while you take a look around and get the things you need."

I nod my head in agreement and head towards my bedroom. I have a huge suitcase I can fit most of my clothes and lingerie into, so I drag it out of the closet.

I'm methodically rolling everything into tight bundles, lost in my thoughts, when he strolls into the room. He immediately goes over to the dresser and grabs the two top drawers. He gives me a wicked grin when he dumps them beside my suitcase. My sleepwear, some of it sheer and risqué, some of it exactly the opposite, flutters down beside the mess of thongs and boy briefs and bralettes. "You've been hiding things, Fierce Girl."

"Just because I haven't invited you to see them doesn't mean I've been hiding them."

"You don't fool me. You're determined to keep anyone from getting too close. For some reason, I'm not one of those people. And you're still in hiding. Unless scotch and darts are involved," he wryly observes.

I blush because he's not wrong. At least the scotch we imbibed together didn't make my clothes fall off. The kiss against the door may have had that effect if he hadn't stepped away, but I'm not about to admit that.

"And now I've made you uncomfortable," he rakes a hand through his wavy hair. "Come on. Let's take your stuff over to my place so you'll feel more settled. I'll drag the guys over here to help me hang up the tarp."

"I really do appreciate it."

"I know, Fierce Girl, I know. But I also know it's hard for you to let people know you appreciate their help since you're not used to asking for it and life has taught you not to expect it."

He sees so easily past my walls. It's disconcerting and yet makes me feel safe. Like nothing I do or say is going to scare him away.

Chapter 15

Sarah

TAREN AND EMMA CORNER me immediately after their arrival.

"I can't say I'm surprised you're shacking up." Emma dryly comments.

I lightly punch her in the arm. "What is that supposed to mean?"

"Well that was some heated exchange in the booth yesterday. And he can't keep his eyes off you. Like you're his personal version of Napoleon's Tina. And you're not doing a good job of hiding your fascination with his enchilada either."

"Maybe I'm just keeping a close eye on the enemy."

She snorts. "Taren, can I please get a witness? Our girl is in straight-up denial."

Taren raises her hands in a gesture of surrender. "I'm not one to judge because I lived in a glass house for so long regarding Zane."

"Whatever," Emma rolls her eyes. "Although you aren't lying. Sarah, you need to work on your game face."

My hands go defensively to my hips. "I have a better game face than the two of you. Especially you," I point a finger in Emma's direction.

"I would have agreed with you before Blake Armitage came rolling into town with his sexy scruff and motorcycle. I've never seen you so ruffled," she teasingly observes.

"I'm not ruffled." I'm not. I'm irritated.

"Not to jump in the middle, but you definitely are," Zane butts in, sliding his arm around Taren's waist like he's permanently attached to her hip and can't stand to be in the same room for more than five minutes without touching her.

I glare at him. "No one asked for commentary from the peanut gallery."

He holds his hand up in a gesture eerily similar to Taren's of a few minutes ago. "Methinks she doth protest too much." Couplehood is turning them into Minions.

"Grrr," I bare my teeth and scowl at the three of them. I don't know why their comments are burrowing underneath my skin. I stomp into the house, the echoes of their laughter in my ears. I know they're teasing me because they care about me, but I feel like I'm going to splinter apart at any second. I'm convinced splashing cold water on my face will restore my calm.

I use the kitchen sprayer to mist my face and take deep breaths. I'm looking out the window, watching Zane and Taren's backyard antics. They brought squirt guns and are chasing each other around the perimeter of the flower beds. I smile. I want that easy camaraderie. Someday. Definitely not today. Today is too soon.

A pair of strong arms wends around my waist. I didn't even hear his footsteps. I know it's him from the smell that wafts across me. I close my eyes briefly. His smell is like cool water. It's almost as calming as the water itself. But I swear he's like a stalking panther. "Did you take lessons on how to sneak up on gazelles or something?" I ask. I want to sound disgruntled and grumpy, but I know I don't.

I'm annoyed because the way he's wrapping himself around me makes me feel safe. He nuzzles aside my hair. "Yes. Because I'm the secret jedi of darts."

"Ummm, yeah... that has nothing to do with your stalking skills." I can't hold back my smile. I snort delicately in response.

"Maybe not, but it sounded good in my head. Besides, I like you thinking of me as a jedi," he whispers into my ear. "Are you okay, Fierce Girl? I haven't known Emma long, but I think she can be pretty ruthless when she wants to be. I didn't mean for them to gang up on you and I don't want you to feel beholden to me, or obligated. You're here because you need a place to stay, and I think we're at least friends. I'd like to think I'm your knight in shining armor and someone you are beginning to trust, not as someone trying to take advantage of you when you're vulnerable. I would never push for more than you're willing to give."

His confession rattles me. Why does he always have to say exactly what I need to hear? Why is the reality of him so much better than the playboy I expected when I first met him? "I am beginning to trust you. And it scares me," I admit. "I'm not comfortable around people, and the way you look at me makes me want to tell everyone in my life who told me I was less to take a flying fuck off a cliff."

"I want to push those damn people off the cliff myself," he growls. "I want to crush the bones of anyone who ever made you feel like that. You are more than enough. So much more. You're almost too much."

I close my eyes at his protectiveness. It steals over me like warm honey, full of grace. I can count on one hand the people in my life who have wanted to protect me and stand up for me. "You really do know what to say at exactly the right time."

"Years of practice. I'm a killer across the negotiating table." He's not boasting, just stating fact. "I have a lot of experience putting people in their place."

"According to Taren, you caved pretty easily."

He chuckles against my ear. "Maybe I know when to hold 'em and when to fold 'em."

"So you're a gambler. That explains so much."

"Like what?"

"Like why you don't care if people make assumptions about you. Like why you aren't afraid to take chances. Like why you're so good at hiding what you feel behind that bad boy, playmaker persona."

"I had to learn to keep my cards close to my chest. I think you had to learn to do that too," I feel his lips brush against the wisps of hair laying against my neck and I think about what Taren said about chasing my satisfaction. Am I detached enough to do that without letting him entrench himself in my heart? Am I detached enough to let him go once I get what I want?

"We need to go back out there before they send in a search party or completely destroy the backyard," he lets go of me only to wrap his fingers around mine and tug me behind him.

I feel much calmer. I'm trying to convince myself it was the moment of solitude, not his words or his touch. "Okay."

He glances back at me. "I promise I'll be like glue. I won't let Emma sink her teeth into you again. I'm the only one allowed to do that," he promises with a delicious growl.

My insides clench as I remember what those teeth felt like scraping against my skin. I follow him outside, pushing my errant thoughts into a box and mentally tossing the key.

Not five minutes later, Emma throws herself into the lounge chair beside mine. "I'm sorry if I hurt your feelings, love," she gruffly murmurs.

I twist in my chair so I can see her expression. "Was that an apology?"

Her lips twist in a mischievous grin. "Not exactly. I know I can push too hard sometimes. But I think this guy could be good for you."

"Why?" I wonder if she sees more than I've given her credit for.

"I can tell when someone besides me is hiding. No matter how well they think they have it disguised. You might not be running from a physical threat, at least I don't think you are, but you're running from yourself."

"I don't think I realized that until recently."

"Men can be great catalysts for epiphanies. Not all of them welcome," there's an iron in her voice I've never heard her use.

"That's a tactful way of explaining it. My grandpa used to say that men can be like a brick through a glass window. Because they're impatient and incapable of subtlety."

She throws her head back in delighted laughter. "That's the perfect description." We fall into companionable silence, watching Zane and Taren chase each other around the yard with water guns.

By the time everyone says goodbye, the stars are just beginning to emerge from behind the cloud wisps.

Blake throws an arm across my shoulders as we tell them good night. I feel lulled by the good company, the comfort of the burgers and potato salad like a solid weight in my stomach, and the sangria. I don't even try ducking away from the easy camaraderie. Dex's crew is cutting up and removing the tree at the crack of dawn tomorrow morning and then Zane and Dex are helping Blake put up tarps to protect my stuff.

When all the headlights have disappeared into the distance, Blake turns me to face him. "Can I show you something? Since it's not supposed to rain tonight, and the clouds are disappearing?"

I glance up. He's right. The clouds are nearly gone. "Okay."

"Really?" he looks at me in disbelief. "I didn't expect you to agree so quickly. I thought I'd have to convince you."

I shake my head, shy in the face of his enthusiasm. "Wait here. Please," he practically runs back into the house. I lift my glass to my lips and finish the sangria. I'm savoring the taste of the last liquor-soaked peach when he returns.

He has a quilt bundled under one arm. His other hand slips into mine, tugging me down the steps. The graveled path crunches beneath our feet and the smell of the pine around us fills the air. We have the only two cabins on this side of the inlet, and there's not a sound of civilization beyond the tread of our feet for miles. The darkness falls around us soft and still as the last ray of sunset sinks beneath the hills beyond. The bullfrog chorus is pulling out all the stops, and there are at least ten thousand fireflies flickering along the tree line. They look like ghost lights in the faint sheen of mist steadily rising from one of the ephemeral creeks that feeds the lake.

He pulls me to the edge of the pier and lowers himself to set the blanket aside. He stretches his legs in front of him, ankles crossed, and braces his arms behind him on the weathered wood. He tips his head back and together we absorb the star-filled vista. I can barely tell where the line of dark water meets the midnight blue velvet backdrop of the sky. I absorb the stillness, hold it inside me and take a deep, cleansing breath. I carefully lower myself beside him, trying desperately not to give in to my nerves, lose my balance and tumble into his lap. I clasp my arms around my knees and lean forward, resting my chin on them. My sundress skims dangerously close to the top of my thighs and when I turn to face him, his eyes are locked there. His gaze is riveted to the sliver of skin revealed by the drift of my hemline.

"I'm trying to behave myself and not fall on you like a ravenous wolf. You have no idea how much I want to bite that sleek, juicy, muscled thigh," he turns his head and shakes it. "But we came out here for stargazing. I hope you love it as much as I do."

"I do love it. To this day, one of my favorite birthday presents of all time was the telescope I received when I turned twelve. My big sister was taking an astronomy class and taught me to recognize all the constellations," I explain.

"Another reason we're two halves of a coin." He gives me a pointed look. "One of my very last foster homes was really close to the state observatory. They had free admission on Fridays and Saturdays, and it was my escape. Searching for comets and exploding stars was a temporary distraction from my struggles. This is the first time in my life I've lived somewhere there isn't a streetlight on every corner. You can see the stars so clearly here. They look close enough to touch. And the Orionid meteor shower is going on right now."

"I didn't know you grew up in foster care," I murmur. I'm surprised. From everything I've heard about him, I thought he grew up with a silver spoon permanently wedged between his teeth.

"And I didn't know you have an older sister," he observes.

"Had," I clarify. Remembering Beth, and her love of space, and how excited she was to share that love with me, brings me to tears.

"Had? Is she someone I'm allowed to ask about?"

"Maybe someday," my response is muffled by the tears choking it down. Those golden eyes are probing me, and I can tell he knows I'm suddenly raw with the need to mourn my loss. I need to change the subject.

"What about you? Are you comfortable talking about growing up in foster care?"

He sighs heavily. "I've learned to be comfortable. I've finally accepted that finding myself in foster care wasn't my fault. That I didn't have some deficit and I was deserving of the love I should've received from my sole remaining parent after my dad was crushed in the middle of a dusty racetrack. I've learned to process my trauma and accept that my mom was dealing with her own demons and depression and it's not my fault she left," he turns to face me, resting his chin against his fist. "After Dad's tragic death, Mom used drugs to self-medicate her highs and lows. She was an opioid addict before it was even recognized as a thing. I was in some wonderful homes and some that weren't so wonderful. Some people take in kids because they truly want to give them a safe, loving place to flourish. And some people do it for the extra money and line their pockets while neglecting the kids that are putting it there. Kids with special needs really struggle. And a lot of us have special needs. It can be one of the reasons we were dumped by our parents in the first place," his voice is rusty with memories.

"I'm sorry you ever felt unwanted and unloved," I may not have known him long, but I can tell he is someone who cares deeply, even if he tries to hide it, and he deserves that in return. "I'm glad you finally recognize that your mom's neglect wasn't because you were unworthy, but because she was incapable," I reach out and lay my hand on his arm. "You said we. Do you have siblings?"

"Just one. My little sister Ellery. She's in grad school at Notre Dame, getting her doctorate in bioengineering. She's on the scale, and none of the homes she was in were equipped to meet the needs of a neglected, neurodivergent kid. As soon as I was old enough, I made sure she had a safe home with me and all the resources she needed. I've made my peace with our past, as much as I can. I have dark days. I just try to focus on giving the energy and care I want to receive. I was angry, and that made me rebellious. I struggled in school because of undiagnosed dyslexia, and probably would've dropped out of high school if it hadn't been for sports."

I'm processing his words. They explain so much about why he's such a walking contradiction. Like me, he's struggled with self-doubt and the feeling that he has to prove himself to people that seem oblivious to his success. He's compelled to be a nurturer, to solve problems because he had to agonize over the lack of care he and his sister received from the system that was supposed to be their safety net. It's why I'm drawn to him – there's so much I would never need to explain because he would get it immediately.

I'm so absorbed by my thoughts; I almost miss it. "Look," I point toward a streaking meteor. "Make a wish."

"I think my wishes are finally coming true," he murmurs. "Maybe I just need to wish they don't dissolve into thin air or aren't pulled out from under me."

When I turn towards him, his gaze is focused on the stars again. I take a deep breath and decide to share a part of my struggle as well. "My social anxiety hasn't always been this pronounced. Something happened to me five years ago that sent me spiraling, and combined with my sensory processing disorder, it can be overwhelming for some people. It's why I don't really date."

"I asked Zane and Dex about you the day we met. They just said you were basically unapproachable and uninterested. But I didn't see that. I could tell you were nervous and agitated when we met – that's one of the reasons I was flirting with you besides the obvious one. I wanted to put you at ease, or at least give you an interaction to focus on. You remind me of Ellery in a lot of ways, and I can tell you've come up with your own coping mechanisms."

"The obvious reason?" I want him to say it instead of hinting at it.

He angles his whole body toward me and holds the quilt out so he can slide it around my shoulders. "The obvious reason is that I knew from the moment I saw you I wanted to belong to you in some way. I don't believe in love at first sight, but it was like I got struck by lightning."

All I can do is sit there in shocked silence. "That's some first impression," I finally observe.

Chapter 16

Blake

I CAN SENSE HER withdrawing. "I didn't mean to make you uncomfortable again."

I turn my head away to gaze up at the stars. There's an awkwardness between us now, and I could kick myself for being so forthright. I told her I knew when to hold my cards and when to fold them. That I was a gambler. And I think I just moved prematurely, and she wasn't prepared to counter it. Usually I hold my cards closer to my chest, but apparently she's the catalyst and I forget what the word chill even means when I'm around her. Now I know exactly what Zane was talking about when he said Taren gave him word vomit. I'm an extrovert, but I don't ever talk about things like this. I feel like I just gave her one of my lungs. I need to repair the damage.

"Do you know anything about the constellation Cassiopeia?" I ask quietly.

"Only that she was the mother of Andromeda, and famous for her vanity. I think I read Bulfinch's mythology at least twenty times in the eighth grade. I wanted to go to Greece and look for Olympus."

"I love those stories too. I think they're what made me love astronomy. I love that the mythology of the Cassiopeia constellation is tied up in the story of a beautiful princess chained up and at the mercy of a sea dragon. One of the houses I stayed in for a while when I was twelve had the original *Clash of the Titans* movie on VHS. I swear I watched it at least fifteen thousand times. It was the original monster romance, even if the monster didn't get the girl," she blushes, and I know she's picked up a few where the monster does get the girl. "The constellation is special too. One of the stars, Cassiopeia A, is a supernova remnant. It's the brightest astronomical radio source in the sky outside our solar system." I twist around to face her. She doesn't turn her head, so I just soak in her profile. "You're my Cassiopeia A. Your brilliance dims everything else. When you're in a room, you're my lodestone. You ground me, but you're also all I can focus on."

She shakily inhales. The whistle of it through her lips makes me feel raw, like she can see my open wounds and my need to have her cauterize them. Like she can see that I want her to be the end of my journey. A journey I didn't even know I was on until I moved to Willow Creek. Until I met her.

"You barely know me," she comments breathlessly. "But if it's true, and not one of your terrible pick-up lines, that's the most amazing thing anyone's ever said to me."

"It's not a pick-up line. You're beautiful because every-thing you are shines through. You try like crazy to hide your light. But I see it. I see the beauty on the inside, even when you're grumpy and sarcastic. Your friends talk about how you're the glue that binds them together, that you might not say much or go out much, but when you do it's to support them. Taren and Emma have already dragged me aside and had the talk. They threatened to cover me in honey, throw me in a trunk and then toss me out where there have been Sasquatch sightings if I make you cry even one tear. I'm pretty sure they were serious."

She must know her friends have just that much crazy in their souls, because she laughs softly and shakes her head. "That's obviously some threat Emma came up with. She reads too much true crime and has a lurid imagination. I mean, do Sasquatch even like honey? Are they even carnivorous?"

"I have no idea. I don't even think I believe in them. But they were both looking at me with deadly intent. There was no way the threat of revenge could be mistaken for anything else. So of course I promised I would avoid hurting you at all costs. Which means you're stuck with me. Even if you never want anything more than friendship."

"What if I haven't made up my mind to let you in? Let alone keep you?"

I hear the confusion in her query. "Like I told you at Guy's, I'm not going anywhere. I'm finally putting down roots because I've never had them. I want them. And I want them here. If I have to wait, or I have to convince you, or both, then I'll do it. I'll do my damnedest to convince you and I'll wait for you to choose me. Even if we're old and gray."

"I just don't understand. Why me? Why here? Why now?"

"I don't understand why. I just know that's how I feel. This place just makes the emptiness I've carried around inside me go away. It's not filled yet, but it no longer aches."

"So maybe I'm not the secret ingredient to your eternal happiness," she observes. "Don't you need to find it in yourself first?"

"I'm on that journey as well. But I also think you're my linchpin. I trust my intuition, and it's telling me you are."

"I don't know if I've ever been both someone's lodestone and their linchpin. What are you going to do to convince me that I'm your saving grace?" She asks, quietly curious.

"We'll start with this," I reach my hand into the space between us and rest my knuckles on the pier, palm open. She slides the slim length of her fingers against my callouses and tangles our fingers together. I remember the promise I made to myself after we almost had angry sex. I promised myself I would let her take the next step and choose me. She just took the first step.

We sit there and watch the swath of stars and the flutter of bats dipping low to catch mosquitoes, and the twinkling of fireflies through the trees, and it's enough for now.

# Chapter 17

Sarah

WE WENT TO OUR separate rooms last night. I had night-mares about the gleam of light off the barrel of the pistol, how it felt to get shoved aside. I woke up shivering and sweating, the sheets and quilt a gnarled mess at the bottom of the bed. I haven't had the dream in months, and I know it's because I wanted to talk about her last night. About how a part of me still thinks it's my fault she won't ever be able to sit on the porch in a rocking chair or help her daughters pick out their wedding dressed. About how it's my fault she won't be there to watch her daughters grow up. About how a part of me blames myself for the grief that splintered our family apart. I haven't spoken to anyone from home in five years. Not since I climbed out that church window and left everything and everyone behind. Because I know they all blame me for what happened. Even if I no longer believe the blame is mine.

It's true that if I had been more aware, if I had reported the creepy emails and the weird presents that kept showing up on the hood of my car, she might still be here. But there's no guarantee that would've prevented it from happening. Police seem to be notorious for ignoring stalker reports from women. They probably would've patted me on the head and placated me by telling me I was being hysterical. But maybe they would've taken me seriously and she would've been the one to point out Cassiopeia and tell me about the Orionic meteor shower. Instead some guy who looks like he could carry me off to his pirate ship anchored somewhere in the Caribbean pointed it out.

And told me I was his radio signal. The distrustful demon on my shoulder tells me he was just feeding me a line, while the angel on my other shoulder hasn't stopped swooning.

I tiptoe my way into the kitchen. It's Sunday and suddenly I want to make us French Toast for breakfast and ask him to go out in the canoe with Sasha and me. He dismantled some of my walls last night, and I don't feel as nervous about spending time with him. It doesn't feel like we're dating, but I can see myself dating him. It's in the realm of possibility, which is a step I haven't considered taking since I threw my wedding dress in a dumpster.

I'm fixing our plates when I hear a yawn so loud, I'm surprised the house isn't shaken from its foundation. It reverberates through the room like King Kong pounding his chest on top of the Empire State Building. I turn around and Blake's standing in the doorway, his arms stretched over his head. I almost drop the plate I'm holding. It's the first time I've seen the tattoos on his chest and arms. The one on his chest is a griffin with a giant sword in its beak. Its wings arch towards his neck, the feathers delineated against his throat and brushing over his ribs and around to his back. There are what look like Viking runes etched on his biceps. He doesn't just look like a pirate; he looks like one of the scourges of the North that convinced the Irish monks to hide all their gold. A legit marauder with a battleax in one hand, standing at the helm of a longboat. A lock of sandy hair covers one eye, and when he sweeps it out of the way, his gaze on me is like bronze topaz.

I look away, wishing my hands were free. "I made us breakfast," I lamely explain. Trying to distract myself from that landscape of golden temptation.

"It smells amazing. That's what woke me up. How'd you know French toast is my favorite?" He's a frisky puppy ready to pounce.

"French toast is everyone's favorite. Or at least it should be. I'm glad you woke up hungry."

"I always wake up hungry," he smirks, and runs his gaze over my flannel pajamas. I thought they were pretty concealing, but he's looking at me like they're transparent or he has x-ray vision. I thrust his plate toward him. "Then dig in."

"Oh, I intend to," my whole body heats up and I turn around and fuss with my own plate.

"I didn't mean to make you blush, O Fierce One. I promise I'll behave if you hand me the syrup."

I try to hand it over, but he pulls me forward. He places a kiss on my forehead and turns away to seat himself at the table.

My forehead is burning where his lips touched it. He keeps doing that and I melt more every time. I busy myself preparing my plate and seat myself across from him. The breakfast nook barely accommodates his sprawl along the bench. "French toast is definitely my favorite," he mumbles around a forkful of food. His eyes are closed in bliss.

Since he can't see me doing it, I take the opportunity to feast on the view of his tattoos. I really want to see what the tattoo on his back is, but I don't want him to catch me trying to get a glimpse. Maybe if we go out in the canoe today he'll strip down to his swimming trunks, and I can see what it is without ogling him.

"So I was thinking we could take the canoe out and go fishing. We don't have that many nice days left before it gets too cold, and the bass and catfish stop biting."

He opens his eyes, and I can't decipher anything there past admiration. "You're full of surprises, Fierce Girl."

"Of course I am, Shark," I go the counter and refill our coffee mugs. "So? Are we on? Do you know how to fish? With a nickname like Shark, you must have some skills," I plop his mug down in front of him. I assumed he knows how to fish. If he doesn't, I can always teach him. With his checkerboard childhood, maybe he never had the chance to learn. He laughs. "Yes, woman, I know how to fish. Although Shark is a recent nickname, bestowed on me by this woman I can't get out of my head. So it's probably not an accurate way of gauging my experience."

"I can't believe I'm the first person to ever call you that. But I'm glad I won't have to spend precious catching time teaching you how to bait and cast," I smirk over at him. "I have some nightcrawlers in a cooler in the garage and two poles leaning against the wall. And my canoe wasn't harmed by the tree catastrophe."

He rubs his hands together, his gaze sparkling. "I fish almost as well as I play darts," he gleefully informs me.

"Is everything a competition with you?" I ask in disbelief. I usually make things a competition too, even if I never say it out loud. It's rare that I meet someone who's as determined to win as I am, no matter what they're doing.

"Only with you. I like exposing the cracks in your composure."

"Ha! I don't believe that. You wouldn't be such a hot shot CEO if that was the case. You thrive on winning as much as I do. And you have your work cut out for you, because I'm not so shabby at fishing myself. So don't get too confident," I warn as I dig into my toast.

"Bring it on," he challenges. "There's only one kicker. We have to be back around two. Dex and Zane are coming over to help me put up the tarps. The tree should be gone by then. I already heard chainsaws."

He seems less and less like the rich playmaker I thought he was. He's loyal to his friends and doesn't mind hard work. "You're not at all who I thought you'd be," I hope he knows that's a compliment. I was prepared to think the worst of him.

"And who is that?" he asks as he comes over to put his plate and cup in the sink and lean his hip against the counter.

"I thought you would look down on the community. We don't have opera or museums. We drive trucks and go fishing and like barn dances."

"Why would I need those things? Do I seem like I'm not content without them here? Do I look like the kind of guy who listens to opera? I just told you about my childhood. I've always been more like the kind of guy who's partial to barn dances."

I look at him quizzically. "You might not be a fan of Pavarotti or Callas, but I think you probably clean up really well and are used to bespoke suits and five-star Michelin dining. I'll admit you've surprised me. I've seen you bantering in the hardware store. I've seen you coaching your team. I've seen the way you fit seamlessly into our circle of friends, like you were a missing puzzle piece..," I trail off, reluctant to say the rest.

"And?" He crosses those muscled arms over his chest.

"And I don't know how I feel about all that. I think it makes it easier for me to trust you – when I have never ever let down my guard this quickly for anyone. Especially a guy who should be an outsider yet seems woven into the very fabric of my life."

He yanks on the bun at his nape in frustration, loosening it. Some of those waves tumble over his forehead and it's like a bright splash of afternoon sun against the cool morning light coming through the kitchen window. "I can't argue with what you're saying, but I can't help how I feel. And how I make you feel. Willow Creek lets me be myself in a way I've never felt comfortable doing anywhere else. There aren't any expectations here beyond what I'm willing to give. I don't have to put on a mask or pretend to be something I'm not. I don't have to strive for something I don't really want because someone else decided that's what I should strive for if I want to be successful. I can be who I want to be here. Who I've always wanted to be."

"And who is that?" I quietly ask.

"It's someone who's fascinated by this amazing woman who turns him more upside down every single day. It's someone who wants to watch her face in the moonlight and hold her hand across the bow of a canoe and show her that he is a better fisherman."

He slides in that last boast with a teasing smile I'm helpless to resist. "I can't wait to kick your butt. I religiously watched all the PBS fishing shows with my grandpa. And he taught me his bass whisperer secrets. You don't stand a chance," I assure him.

"So another competition, then?" he eagerly asks.

"Yeah, why not?"

"Same prize as last time?" His eyes don't leave my face. I can sense that if my answer is yes, they'll be filled with determination.

"Okay," I acquiesce. "A kiss, right? No matter who wins?"

"Hell, yes," he pumps a fist in the air. "But how do we know who wins? Is it which one of us catches the most fish or which one of us catches the biggest fish?"

"It's going to be whichever one of us catches the biggest fish," I decide. "We're doing catch and release for the rest. I don't feel like scaling and deboning a whole mess of fish tonight."

"See, I knew you were the kind of woman that wouldn't get voted off the island," he grins and gives me a thumbs up.

"I'm definitely not cut out for all that crap, especially under the microscopic examination of a camera and thirty million viewers," I shiver in disgust. I've always hated public scrutiny, and that would even be worse than the televised matches because it would live forever on the streaming platforms. "You can thank my erstwhile Girl

Scout leaders and my Gramps. They taught me everything I need to survive in case the zombie apocalypse Taren's obsessed with ever actually happens."

"Zane thinks her obsession is adorable. They're spending the morning adding to their bugout bags. He texted me a picture of the dining room table full of fire starters and MREs. I never thought I'd see the day that he was so head over heels."

"She's definitely watched *The Book of Eli* and *The Walking Dead* too many times, and she's always asking our opinions about new inventions designed for wilderness survival," I agree, chuckling.

I don't have the chance to turn away or protest when he bends down and pecks my cheek. "Thanks for breakfast. Definitely not what I expected when you agreed to be my roomie," his arms go around my waist and he gives me a brief, warm hug. "I'm throwing on some clothes and we're going fishing," he yells over his shoulder as he jogs away.

I'm not even going to try and figure out what he expected when I agreed to be his roomie. I take a deep breath and finish washing the dishes in the sink. I'm going to try dwelling on something besides touching those tattoos. Or licking them.

Chapter 18

Blake

WE ROWED IN PERFECT tandem, right away. I haven't done crew since my freshman year of high school, but the muscle memory is still there. I matched her strong, certain oar strokes and we sliced through the water like the wings of a swan, leaving barely a ripple over the smooth surface. We headed for the middle of the lake, watching the shorebirds and a flock of mallards in the soft mid-morning light. The sky is a clear, cloudless, cyan that meets the moss green vista stretching in front of us.

She's wearing an old t-shirt tied in a knot at her hip, cutoff jeans that barely cover the tops of her thighs, and Birkenstocks. And her ponytail is sticking out the back of her baseball cap. She looks comfortable and fresh-faced, and I want to play connect the dots with the dusting of freckles across her nose and cheekbones. I love the fact that she doesn't wear makeup beyond lip gloss and a touch of mascara, and even that's absent today. She's completely in her element, basking in the warm sunlight of early autumn. Her fishing pole is secured beside her and she's leaning back, her face tipped upwards. She hasn't said much since we left the house, and I'm okay with that.

My pole jerks and I scramble out of my daydreams to reel it in. It's bent at an almost right angle, and I'm confident this is my winning catch. A minute later, a ten-pound bass is flopping on the deck. I scoop it into the bucket and grin at her. "Looks like I'm in it to win it," I tease.

"Hah! Lucky catch. Remember I'm the Bass Whisperer," she reminds me.

"We'll see. I win either way because the prize is those lips."

She's still blushing when her fishing rod nearly gets pulled from the holster. Now she's the one scrambling. She braces her feet and reels it in. I want to stand behind her for balance or support or whatever she needs, but she obviously doesn't need or want my help. When her catch lands on the deck, she gives me a triumphant smile that would knock me flat with its brightness if I wasn't already reclining against the edge of the boat.

I glance down at the fish flopping around like mad. It's more than twice the size of my catch. A monster flathead catfish with whiskers almost the length of my arm.

"You may as well concede defeat," she arches her brow at me.

"Never. I will go down fighting," I assure her.

We both have a bucketful of fish in less than an hour. She's still the winner by a long shot. Nothing either of us has caught in the last hour has even come close to the size of her catfish.

"So we're having fried catfish with remoulade tonight," I inform her.

"You're full of surprises, Shark. I didn't know you could cook as well. Turnabout is fair play, anyway. I made breakfast so dinner is all on you," her gaze is teasing but appreciative.

"You get tired of Door Dash when you live alone. Watching The Food Network and HGTV is how I relax. We're going to binge *Cajun Aces* so I can convert you."

"You're making me Cajun?" her eyes light up. "Consider me converted already if you're volunteering to feed me dinner. Especially if it's Cajun. And if you tell me you can make a mean jambalaya I may just shack up with you forever."

"I think my jambalaya's pretty mean – you may be eating your words."

We throw all the fish back but her winning quarry. "I'll do everything since you won. Including deboning, scaling, and fileting it."

"Well it's a good thing you volunteered, because I was going to conscript you for clean-up duty anyway."

"Maybe you'd better claim your prize before we get back and I'm otherwise occupied," I casually propose.

"I think I'll wait. I want to claim it when you least expect it."

The guys haven't started ribbing me yet, but I know it's inevitable. Zane has been smirking since he walked in and caught me watching Sarah's ass in her cut-off shorts. Dex just gave me a very pointed look and shook his head. And I'm pretty sure he muttered, "Another one bites the dust."

I climb the ladder first, the gigantic tarp rolled up under my arm. Zane and Dex are close on my heels. I whip it out and it covers almost the entire roof. I sigh in relief. The look on her face when she saw the devastation in full daylight ripped my heart in half. I want to make sure none of the rest of her stuff gets ruined while we're waiting on the repair crew.

Zane and Dex both have staple guns, and we've secured the cover in way less time than I expected. We're back on the ground again, hands on our hips surveying our work, when Zane finally turns to me. "Admit it, Bro."

I decide to feign ignorance. "Admit what?"

"You're a goner. Tickets to the last light show were sold a long time ago."

"You're one to talk."

"I chased my happiness with Taren, and I hope you do the same thing with Sarah. There's no shame in running after the woman you want to spend your forever with," he chides me.

"I never thought this would happen to me. Especially not some place like Willow Creek," I admit.

"It's a lot more than it seems, and the women here have a way of getting under a man's skin and hanging his heart out to dry," rumbles Dex.

It's an accurate assessment, and there's no point in refuting it. "Half the time I feel like a fifteen-year-old on his first date. The other half the time I feel like I'm walking barefoot over a bed of hot coals."

"Welcome to my world," Zane slaps me between the shoulder blades. "Now I do stuff like watch her while she's sleeping, reassuring myself she's really lying beside me and it's not my imagination playing tricks on me. And I can't stop my heart from lodging in my throat every time she leaves my side, hoping and praying she'll come back to me safe and in one piece and still love me as much as she does now," he sighs. "It's a lot. And it's brutal and wreaks daily havoc on me, but it's also totally worth it."

"And this is why I'm still single," Dex smugly informs us.

"Whatever, dude. If that curvy doctor ever gave you the time of day, you'd be in the same boat. Don't even try to deny it," Zane scoffs. "I don't know what happened between the two of you in that desert, but I know it scarred you for life. More deeply and permanently than the air raid that landed you in rehab for almost a year. Someday I hope you'll let down your guard enough to tell me the whole story," he finishes, and clasps Dex on the shoulder.

"I guess the moral of the story is that this town and these women have the power to shred a man's soul and turn everything he thought he knew about himself completely upside down," I observe.

"Yeah, that's one way to explain it," Zane ruefully agrees.

"The Marines shredded me enough already, I don't need any more nightmares," Dex warns.

"Dex, man, you may not have any choice in the matter whatsoever. When it's meant to happen, it's going to happen and you're going to feel like your kayak got caught in a whirlpool and you lost your paddle. When it happens – and it will – don't bother fighting it. Just surrender and enjoy the adventure," Zane advises.

"Well now is not my time," Dex glares at both of us. "It's this asshole's," he points in my direction. "And he has a woman to woo with his grilling game and stories of missions involving tarps accomplished."

"So far it's been an uphill battle," I run my hands though my hair and lift my chin in the direction of the sky. "She's deadset against jumping into anything that reeks of more than right now."

"Taren was the same way," Zane rubs his chin thoughtfully. "Actually, I think Sarah was the one who gave her the advice to live in the moment and 'chase your orgasms.' So maybe she's taking her own advice and pushing you away unless she decides she needs to scratch an itch," he concludes.

"It's driving me crazy! Just when I think I'm getting underneath her defenses, she pushes me away again. She's vulnerable and open, and then she's an ice queen again."

"Give her time. That's the best advice I can offer," Zane offers. "I'm sure you already know this, but that crap that works on the shallow gold-diggers in the city doesn't work on these women. They're not going to open up unless you do it first."

I mull over what Zane's telling me. "I don't like wearing my heart on my sleeve," I confess. "But I told her last night she was my Cassiopeia A and I think it terrified her."

"I don't even know what that is. Why would it terrify her?" Zane asks in puzzlement.

"It's the star with the strongest radio signal," I solemnly inform them.

Zane gives a low whistle. Dex sighs and gives me a pitying look. "If that didn't sway her, you really do need us to pray for you."

"Just keep telling her stuff like that," Zane advises. "You have no choice in the matter if you want to keep her. She's not going to give you her heart unless she knows you've given yours first. She knows she's perfectly fine by herself, that she's strong and capable. She doesn't need you to survive. You have to convince her you're worth it anyway. That you'll make her life fuller instead of becoming just another person or thing she has to worry about or regret."

"That bar seems basically insurmountable," I lament.

"That's why it feels like you're standing on top of the world when you finally get there," Zane's eyes turn misty. "I felt like I'd won a gold medal and been the first person on the moon and faced down Genghis Khan with nothing but my fists and my teeth. Nothing compares to it. Nothing," he finishes fiercely.

Chapter 19

Sarah

WINNING OUR BET MADE me giddy. Which makes no sense because the prize was the same no matter who won. I'm giddy that he's cooking me dinner. I only see the world in rose-gold undertones, like I drank the Kool-Aid and am wearing the shades, because I'm giddy over the undercurrents I sense moving between us. He's effortlessly creeping beneath my defenses and making me question why I was so resistant to an actual relationship. Especially when I can laugh without reservation, revel in the simple joy of his presence, and look forward to every single moment, stolen or otherwise. He sets something loose in my chest that's been coiled there for so long I forgot it existed. I thought I was going to cry when he told me I was his Cassiopeia A. It took every ounce of my self-control to hide how that affected me.

I'm irrationally excited about claiming that kiss, about making him want me so much he can't keep his hands to himself or the growls from escaping. I want to unfurl that bun at his nape and nibble every inch of those tattoos. We're just roomies, I keep telling myself. Even though I've caught him sniffing the nape of my neck. Even though roomies don't lend each other their weighted blankets and snuggle with you on the couch. Even though roomies don't try to make friends with your dog that wants nothing to do with them. At least none of my college roomies or teammates wanted to do any of those things. But he obviously does. And that makes him more than a roomie, more than a friend. I've never had such easy camaraderie with a guy, and I don't know what that means.

I took a quick shower to slough off the sweat and put on another pair of comfy, stretchy cutoffs and a tank while he and the guys were putting up the tarps. They pulled out a few minutes ago and left us to ourselves. I adamantly tell myself I'm not dressing to catch his attention or admiration. I don't even blow dry my hair. It's held back from my face in a loose bun with one of my softest bookish scrunchies. I just wanted it out of my way so I can help cut vegetables or whatever. So it doesn't look like I'm too eager to lend my assistance in the kitchen, or too eager about claiming my prize for hauling in the biggest catch of the day.

I am going to be nothing more than a casual observer. When I finally creep into the kitchen, he's standing there shirtless. And I can see the tapestry on his back in all its glory. It's the Celtic serpent with its tail in its mouth, the symbol of eternity. It's been drawn to resemble a dragon, with papery wings and flames coming out of its nostrils. I dig my nails into my palms, so I won't trace it with my fingers and then lick it like a lunatic. Even though I'm trying to be stealthy, he either hears or senses my entrance.

"I had to toss the shirt because, hello, fish guts," he informs me with a grin over his shoulder.

I grimace. "Blech. Least appealing part of catching your own dinner. You'll never know how glad I am you're the one that lost our fishing contest."

His laughter filters through the kitchen with unbridled joy, like the bells from the steeple on Christmas morning. I've only heard him chuckle before. This is a full out belly laugh and I want to inhale it. "You're lucky I don't mind because I'm looking forward to my consolation prize," he cockily informs me.

"Maybe I like making you wait. What makes you think I'm going to claim it tonight, Shark?" I'm totally claiming it tonight. There's no way I can spend another restless night trying to remember how his lips feel against mine. But I will never admit my weakness.

"I think you're just as stoked and edgy as I am, but I'm not going to press you. I'll wait for it as long as I have to. The next move is yours," he assures me.

"Well, I'll make it when you least expect it."

"Of that I have no doubt," he winks.

It should be annoying, but it's not. It's sexy as hell. I am in so much trouble. "So I wanted to see if you needed help with anything? I thought you might like to jump in the shower and wash off the sweat?" I don't really want him to wash off the sweat. I can smell it even over the fish. Which should be grossing me out but somehow isn't. I think I might be like Drew Barrymore from *50 First Dates*.

"You can go ahead and toss together a salad. The fish is already seasoned and I'm just going to pop it in the oven. All the ingredients you need should be in the crisper since I restocked at the farmer's market," he rinses his hands and then grabs the pan and slides it onto the oven rack.

"I can do that. I can watch the main course too. How long should I set the timer for?"

"Just thirty minutes. And that'll give me plenty of time to make myself presentable."

I walk forward at the same time he does, and we're trapped against each other in the open doorway. Being that close to his skin, and smelling his sweat up close overwhelms me. I want to press my nose against his collarbone. The usual notes of amber and earth and cedar are both muted and enhanced. I jolt away when I'm seconds from burying my entire face against the crevice between his neck and shoulder. "I'll let you get to it, then," I croak as I slide past him.

He gives me a knowing look. "I'm looking forward to that kiss, Fierce Girl. You can't avoid the sparks between us forever."

I blush and turn around so he can't see it.

"So looking forward to it," he calls out as he bounds up the stairs.

I focus on shredding the lettuce and slicing the onions, tomatoes, and cucumbers. The alarm goes off just as I'm finishing up, and I use his gigantic oven mitts to pull out the fish. It looks delicious, and I can smell the lemon and cumin he used. I can't identify the other seasonings.

When he joins me again I almost dissolve into a puddle where I stand. He's in a sleeveless cotton tank and gray sweatpants. The runes on his arms seem to glow. I take a deep breath and try to focus on our meal. The table is set, and the white wine has been poured. "I hope it's okay that I helped myself to the wine rack. I thought we deserved it."

"Absolutely. And I already told you, when I said *mi casa es su casa* I meant it," he steps forward and clasps my hands. I didn't even realize I was twisting them in front of me. I do it a lot in his presence. "I want you to feel completely comfortable here, and never question whether there's something you should or shouldn't be doing or something you should leave alone. I think I've told you most of my secrets and I hope someday you'll trust me enough to tell me yours," he leans forward and presses a kiss to my forehead. That's at least three forehead kisses in the span of less than twenty-four hours. Something melts inside me each time he does it, and I think he knows it.

I know he meant to relieve my anxiety, but his words twine around me, and I feel myself plummeting toward certain destruction. My mind goes into protection mode, skittering away from any analysis of the things he makes me feel. The things I want to do against my better judgment all involve him. He's the thing I know I should leave alone. I can't let him see all of me, because once I do, he'll leave. I'll be stuck on the side of the road I never should have taken, battered, and bruised and left to pick up the pieces of myself. Again.

"Are you sure you're not a vampire?" I can't help asking, trying to lighten the mood and escape the spiral of my dark thoughts.

"I already told you not to compare me to Edward," he grins.

"You're sure you don't have any special powers of compulsion or anything?" I insist.

"No, Fierce Girl. If you're attracted to me, it's only natural. I'm just getting underneath your skin like you're getting under mine," he asserts.

"You're not exactly the most convenient distraction, Shark," I huff.

"If I was convenient you could put me in one of your boxes and ignore me. But you can't," he smugly replies.

"I really want to kiss you now," I admit.

"If you kiss me now, I'm going to lay you on this table and have a feast of my own," he promises.

An electric shock sweeps through my entire body because his words are brimming with heat. "I probably wouldn't complain," I squeak out like a tiny mouse.

My whole inner avatar is shaking with nerves, but I step forward and put my feet on top of his. That little lift makes us equal in height, and I'm looking straight into his eyes.

"I love the fact that a few inches are all it takes, and I can devour you without even craning my neck," he rumbles.

I loop my arms around his nape and grab the loose tendrils of hair escaping from the band doing a piss-poor job of keeping his hair out of his face. "But it's my turn to devour, not yours," I whisper, and sink my mouth into his.

His hands tighten around my waist, and he groans into the kiss. I feel that vibration against my lips and the tremors it ignites chase over every inch of my skin, covered or not. I moan in response, unable to stifle my reaction to the hunger I sense in his touch.

I push lightly against his chest, one hand still wrapped in his hair, urging him to back up. When his hips are finally resting against the counter I delve into the kiss in earnest. I lick the cupid's bow of his upper lip, graze my mouth across the dusting of stubble across his cheeks, ferociously nip his earlobe. I press my hips into his and inch a hand under his shirt, finally letting go of his hair. "Off," I command.

His gaze on fire, he yanks off the cotton that's been obscuring my view. I drop my gaze and dance my fingers across every shadow and nuance of the tattoo blanketing his chest. I trace the outline of the griffin and rest my palm against the sword carved over his heart. He shivers at my touch and grinds the bulge of his erection against me. We're perfectly lined up because I'm still standing on his feet. "I think I must excite you," I murmur mischievously.

"Fierce Girl, you know for a fact that's the understatement of the century," he cups the curve of my cheek in his hand. "You excite me. You intrigue me. You captivate me. Every single moment I spend at your side makes me more like a fly flailing against the sticky strands of your web. Or like one already caught on a piece of fly tape, knowing there's no escape and I'm going to starve. I'm scared to death, and I know my demise is coming, but I know I can't get away and trying to escape is both futile and stupid. Because even if this means certain death, it will be the making of me."

The things this man says to me. And on such brief acquaintance. I know we're living on top of each other right now, but that's a newish development. He's been acting like he's known me his whole life. He's so certain of his feelings, so confident of where they're leading him. It makes me wonder if he has a crystal ball or a convenient pack of tarot hidden in a junk drawer somewhere that's giving him clues on how to navigate the murky waters between us.

This time, his lips brush mine. He presses a gentle kiss and licks across their closed seam, begging entry. I grant it and he's hoisting me in the air. "Legs around my waist," he growls. Of course I obey because I want to cling to him like a second skin. I want to feel those calloused, nicked, capable hands with their blunt nails and scraped knuckles resting on my hips. I want to feel his breath catch in my ear, and the rasp of his five 'o'clock shadow against my cheek. He twists us around and now my butt is solidly on the counter, and he's wedged against me.

The silk of his tongue slides against mine, and it's hot and dark.

He twines it around mine, and it's even hotter and darker.

He sucks the end of my tongue into his warmth, showing me without words all its wicked skills and what his intentions are once we're both naked. "Do you feel that?" he asks as he thrusts against me. It's the same angle that had me so close to clambering him against a wall of lockers.

The solid length of him glides across my center, while he worships my mouth. His hands are in my hair and mine are gripping his upper arms, pressed against his biceps so hard I can see the little half-moon indentations of my nails on his skin. He yanks my cutoffs down and lays his palm against the outer curve of my upper thigh. It feels like a brand, and I swear I can hear it sizzling like drops of water flung into a bonfire. I want to be even closer. I rub against his palm and use my heels to pull him more firmly against me. His cock is outlined in extravagant detail against the gray of his sweatpants.

He pulls back and tips up my chin. "Not to be the voice of reason, but we went to all that trouble to catch our dinner, and I've been bragging about my kitchen game. We should eat. Food, not each other. At least not yet," he amends. "We'll need our strength if you're finally letting me into your bed," he's giving me puppy dog eyes, like he's ready to beg for scraps. All hope and optimism and eagerness and even a hint of *I can't wait to show off for you.*

He didn't say anything about his heart, maybe because he knows I can't help my skepticism. He's been laying it on pretty thick, and I know he can tell I don't know how I'm supposed to react. But I can openly admit that my body wants his and his body wants mine, and there's no reason we shouldn't let our bodies decide what's best for us right now. We can figure everything else out later if there's more we need to take into consideration. Right now, I'm thinking he's exactly what I need to lay my anxiety about the storm damage to rest. Consequences be damned. "Yes, I think I'm done trying to resist you. Taren gave me the same lecture I gave her months ago about seizing a prime opportunity. And you are a prime opportunity."

We sit down across from each other. Instead of relishing the immaculate table setting or the divine meal, we shovel our food in like we're trying to leave the school cafeteria as fast as we can and make our recess last longer. The buzz of anticipation fills the air, and he might be an excellent cook, but everything may as well taste like dust. I'm a terrible judge of his skills because I'm so focused on how we'll be spending the rest of the night I barely notice the fork passing my lips or the wine coating my throat. I know it's not making me want to gag or spit it into my napkin, but honestly, nothing registers beyond that. He's sitting there shirtless because he couldn't be bothered to put it back on. And it's hard to concentrate on anything else when all I want to do is follow that trail of dark amber hair with my tongue. To discover if he's as hard and slick against the roof of my mouth as he felt grinding me against the counter.

Where is the rulebook that says we have to use a bed? This table is a flat surface. And it's closer. And way more convenient. Who cares if we break a few dishes? And he said I could take charge and make this happen the way I want it to. I determinedly push the chair back, the legs scraping against the wood floor and stalk towards him.

"Now who's the panther?" he asks.

"That would be me. I can't concentrate on eating right now. Everything just tastes like dust. I want to concentrate on another equally important, but often neglected, need in Maslow's hierarchy."

"Are you getting ready to pounce on me?" he teases.

I don't answer. I just lower myself so I'm straddling his lap. "I wouldn't exactly call this pouncing. More like claiming."

He settles one arm around my waist and raises the other one so he can cup my cheek, his thumb brushing against the freckles scattered across it. His eyes follow the path of his thumb. "Even your freckles are a constellation," he wonderingly observes.

"I don't have enough for them to be a constellation. I'm very diligent about using sunscreen," I correct him.

"Maybe not exactly a constellation," he amends wryly. "Maybe they're more like the tail end of a comet, a little sprinkle of stardust that's been gallivanting around the galaxy for billions of years."

"I think that's a much more accurate description," I intone in my best *you can go to the head of the class* voice.

"So what does this claiming involve?"

He sounds nonchalant, but I can see his impatience simmering beneath the surface of that calm exterior. He's anything but nonchalant. He's letting me set the pace and it's exhilarating. Maybe that's why I've never felt this comfortable with other guys. They were too preoccupied with controlling everything, down to the very last detail. He's just watching me. The only thing that's giving away his nerves is the slight jiggle of his right foot. I like the fact that his body is betraying him, even if it's barely noticeable.

I loop my arms around his neck. "Well, first it involves me inhaling your scent," I bend forward and glide my nose up the column of his throat, setting my open mouth against the bob of his Adam's apple and giving it a furtive lick. His skin tastes like amber and the decadent forest in late fall, when the world is full of decay but still bright and golden. I nip him again and trail my nose up to the spot just behind his right ear. I nuzzle into the space there, like it's a pillow I can't live without and need to hoist beneath my body so I can feel it like a balm against my skin even when I'm sound asleep.

He shivers when I burrow even closer and exhale softly into his ear. "That tickles," he murmurs. But he doesn't pull away. I clamp my front teeth down on his earlobe and dance my fingers lightly against his nape. He shivers again, and I can feel him break into goosebumps beneath my touch. I don't break the skin; I just make sure he knows that I'm claiming him. Not for a forever, but definitely for as long as I'm stuck in this house with him. Because I'm tired of fighting it.

"You smell like what I always wanted Old Spice to smell like. I had this fantasy in my head that it would smell exactly like you, like amber and pirates and adventure. I almost gagged the first time I was around someone who was actually wearing it," I nuzzle behind his other ear.

"That's a very specific fantasy. Pirates and adventure?" he teases.

"Yes. And not like in Pirates of the Caribbean. I'm more of a Black Sails woman. You're like a Johanna Lindsey Malory cover come to life. I have this old copy of *A Gentle Rogue* I inherited from my aunt, and it has Fabio braced on the deck of a ship in an open white shirt, with his hair streaming around him. He's clasping the heroine around the waist, like he's saving her from falling overboard, but is probably about to ravish her." He's watching me with rapt attention. I blush a little, because when I think about that clinch cover and picture him caging me against the prow of a ship, I get extremely swoony.

"That's called a clinch cover."

I shake my head, and there's no way he can miss the way my eyes are shining with approval. "So you've seen them?"

He laughs gruffly. "Have I seen them?" He chuckles again. "Yes, not that particular one, but my little sister is obsessed with them. Every time she's home she drags me into scouring used bookstores with her in search of them."

"You're a very good brother," I praise him.

"I try to be," he somberly replies. "I have a lot to make up for. We got separated when we went into foster care, and she went through some things she never should've had to deal with."

I brush my hand through his wavy hair in a soothing motion. "I'm sorry you couldn't protect her. I think you would've done an amazing job."

He leans forward and rests his head against my shoulder, exhaling slowly. "I think I would have too. Since I didn't get the chance, I've tried to make sure she wants for nothing. Our mom's drug habit impacted how my sister's brain is wired. I know I told you last night that she's on the spectrum. She's always processed things differently than others, and sometimes it's to her detriment through no fault of her own. People can be ignorant and intolerant."

"I didn't think it was possible you could become more attractive," I mutter, mostly to myself. It's true. Every time

I think I couldn't possibly find him more attractive he spills another little revelation.

"I don't think attraction between us will ever be a problem, Fierce Girl. All the hard stuff is what's getting in the way. I feel like I've spilled my guts to you, but you've been keeping your distance."

I lean away and look down. "There are things about my past, about how and why I ended up here, I'm not comfortable sharing yet."

He nods. "I appreciate your honesty and I can respect that. That doesn't change the fact that someday I hope you'll feel comfortable oversharing with me," he smiles gently and brushes my hair to the side.

I nestle more snugly against him. "I still haven't finished claiming you."

"I was hoping this was just a blip in the radar. I'm at your mercy."

I want to jump up and down. I'll finally get to touch and map and lick all his tattoos. "We're going upstairs so you can strip for me."

I jump up and head straight for his bedroom.

"Do I need a Magic Mike routine?" He asks with amusement.

"No," I call over my shoulder as I skid to a stop in front of his door. "But...can I put in a future request?"

"Only if I get a burlesque show too," he growls against my nape and pushes us both through the door.

He nudges me toward the bed. I sit down in the middle of it, bouncing on my knees, my hands clasped under my chin. I can barely contain my excitement. "Please go slowly. I want to savor this."

He laughs again. "Most people want to rip each other's clothes off."

"I may want to do that later. I may even buy you one of those billowy white shirts from one of the Ren Fair sites so I can rip it off with my teeth."

"Savage," he observes. But I can tell he likes it.

He eases the sweatpants down a millimeter at a time. Now they're hanging on his hips. I can see that the tattoo on his back winds around his hip bones, and I want to trace those tendrils of ink with my tongue. He pushes them below the curve of his muscled ass, and now the elastic is keeping them anchored to his thighs. I don't think I can even wrap my hands around them. They're like giant Sequoia trunks. "Wow," I breathe.

He's not commando, but he may as well be. The tip of his erection is peeking through the opening of his boxer briefs, and I lick my lips.

"I'll show you wow, Fierce Girl," he promises.

He pushes the pants all the way off, raising each leg and kicking them away. Like he knows I need a minute to absorb every detail, he puts his hands on his hips. "I think if I looked at you long enough I would forget I need bread and water to survive," I admit.

Chapter 20

Sarah

HE HAS AN EIGHT pack. I didn't even know those existed outside of superhero mythology. I scoot forward. I feel like I'm witnessing the unveiling of Hercules. He could be a lion, but I'm convinced he could also fight lions bare handed.

"Do you want to get more up close and personal?" he teases.

"Yes," I shimmy off the bed and stride toward him. I keep my eyes locked on his as I raise both hands to his chest. "I've wanted to do this since you almost made me drop your plate this morning."

I savor the feel of him, satin skin over hard muscle, and glide my hands back and forth like I'm wielding a paint-brush. Delicate strokes across his collarbones, to capture the fracture of light and shadow that nestles in the hollow of his throat. Broad strokes down from his shoulders, cir-cling the copper coins at his breastbone with my thumb and forefinger. He groans at that touch, and it makes me want to feel his hands on me there. But I'm nowhere near finished with my exploration.

I coast my palms down his sides, bracing them in the en-clave just above his navel, like I went on a long hike without a canteen and I'm dying of thirst, and I don't care that I have to resort to scooping up the dripping water from a lake with my cupped hands. I slide my pointer finger down the arrow that's pointing to Candyland, because this is the one part of his map that needs no explanation. I wonder what will happen when I finally touch him there. What noises he'll make and if he'll get goosebumps on those pirate thighs.

I hope he does. I want to feel them against my tongue, like pebbles, when I chase how all the tattoos connect to each other.

I grip the outer curve of his thighs, deliberately avoiding the part of him I want to cradle in my palms. He reaches around, his hands enveloping my grip. His head is tipped down toward me, his gaze inscrutable, a color wheel like a banked fire. Umber and mahogany and sienna and even a hint of brass and copper. There's knowledge and certainty gleaming in those depths, and I want to shy away from it.

He won't let me shy away. His hands are clenching mine, demanding that I acknowledge what's happening between us is more than a way to expend excess energy, more than a way to let off steam.

I'm not ready to let him define us that way, I don't know if I'll ever be ready. Confronting how I feel, making others confront the way they make me feel, is something I'm still learning how to do. Even though I want to duck my head to avoid letting him see the fear and doubt that's eating me alive, I steadily return his gaze. He moves one of his hands and cups the side of my face, sliding his fingers into my hair and holding my jaw like he would handle spun glass. He nods his head, just once.

He's telling me it's okay to explore him to my heart's content. He's telling me he understands why I'm afraid. He's also telling me he's no longer going to allow me to use my fear as an excuse to keep my distance. He's giving me the final push to let go of the ghosts that have been haunting me since I moved to Willow Creek. He's already banished the ghosts from his past, and he's telling me he'll show me how to do it, that he'll be there to shore me up when I falter, to catch me when I stumble. That unspoken promise, and the devotion behind it, is humbling.

I bow my head to take in the whole of him. His knees and his calves are lean with muscle and feathered with almost translucent whorls of pale moon spun silk. It's slightly coarse against the pads of my fingers when I brush it backwards. I cup the hard slope of tendon behind his shin, kneading the knots I feel there. I brush my hand over the top of his foot, strong and capable. His second toe is longer than his big toe, and I love the asymmetrical imperfection. That imperfection doesn't detract from its lean beauty - the subtle arch just above the heel, the ridges of dorsal muscle that line its top like an army of little wizened gnomes. It has a clean, spare strength that echoes the rest of him.

I circle his ankle, just barely, and trail my fingers up the insides of his thighs. His breath is shallow with anticipation, and he braces his feet slightly, spreading his stance wider. He jerks and gasps when I slide the edge of my thumbnail around the tender skin that lines the rim of his cock.

I draw back to take in his facial expression. He looks like he's about to charge forward onto the beaches of Normandy or yell before he jumps from a plane. He's all stoic male, grim faced with glittering eyes. His neck muscles are corded and rigid with strain and there are faint lines bracketing his mouth because his jaw is clenched so tightly.

I keep my eyes on his and lightly touch the leak of pre-cum. I scoop it up and raise it to my mouth, swallowing my finger and then releasing it with a loud pop and a lick of my lips. He swells even more. "Fuck, don't stop," he groans. "If you're going to do what I think you're going to do."

"Oh, I definitely intend to do that. And I don't have any plans to stop," I assure him. "You're going to be at my mercy, Shark."

"If you mean to destroy me, you're doing a damn fine job of it," he grumbles.

"Slow and easy wins the war," I chide.

"Whatever idiot said that needs to be drawn and quartered. I'll die of anticipation before then," he warns, as he slides his hands into my hair. "Please take me in your mouth," he begs hoarsely.

"Well, you did say please. You should be very grateful right now that someone bothered to teach you the magic words," I tease. "And I like to hear you begging."

His hands tighten in my hair, just a fraction. Silently instructing me to get down to business.

I watch him through half-closed lids as I scoot closer. I raise my left hand and slide it across the top of him before I use it to squeeze the root of his cock. He groans softly again, and I smile slyly in response. Letting him know that this is just the beginning of the torture session I have planned. I watch him as I tighten my grip and move my thumb back and forth, pressing against the ridges. I raise my right arm and wrap it around him, securing the back of his thigh between my neck and shoulder blade, splaying my hand over the sinuous muscles of his ass.

It's been more than five years since I've had a man's cock in my mouth, but there are some things you never forget how to do. I'm about to let his girth test my gag reflexes when he thrusts my chin up and shakes his head.

"Are you kidding me?" I ask in disbelief.

"No," he rumbles. "Not like this. I want to taste you for the first time while you're tasting me," he pulls me up and grabs my hand to lead me toward the bed.

I've never actually done a sixty-nine and I'm more than a little apprehensive about managing the mechanics of it. "I've never actually done this before," I admit.

He drops my hand and turns to face me. "Do you want to do it?"

"Yes, but I'm worried about what I'll look like trying to figure it out. Especially where to put things like my elbows and my knees."

He smiles at me with genuine affection. "You could never look anything less than beautiful because you're giving me the gift of your trust. You're letting me worship you," he drops a kiss on my forehead. "And sex isn't supposed to be perfect. It's supposed to be messy and clumsy and organic. It's supposed to be whatever makes us feel good and I will never judge you for anything that happens between our bodies."

"So you're saying you'll judge me for other things?"

He gives me an indecipherable look. "I'll judge you if you run away or retreat back into your shell like a baby turtle," he brackets my face, forcing me to meet his gaze. "I'll judge you if you deny that what is happening between us is real."

He's asking for more than I've ever given anyone. Even the man I almost married. He's asking me for unconditional surrender. "You're asking for a lot."

"I know," his gaze searches mine. "But I think you're worth it, and I hope you think I am too."

"I'm still trying to wrap my head around this," I flap my hand awkwardly between us like a one-winged stork. "Can we just do this and have fun and take one day at a time?" I plead.

He smiles again. "Yes, we can do this. I'll let you use my body like it's your personal playground."

"I can't wait to frolic on you," I giggle. I clap my hand over my mouth in horror. No man has ever reduced me to giggling. Especially not during the prelude to what may very well be the hottest sex of my life.

He falls backward onto the bed and yanks me down on top of him. I fall across him like a boneless limpet. And of course I immediately try to get my knees and elbows in some semblance of order. His waist is narrow, but his torso and his hips are broad. I huff in frustration. "This is impossible."

"No it's not," he assures me. And then he grabs me by the hips and lifts me over his entire body, twisting me around so all my goodies are in his face, and I can reach out and nudge his cock with my nose.

If my head wasn't still spinning, I'd be melting. Who am I kidding? I'm melting. I never dreamed a maneuver like that would turn me on so much I can't think clearly or catch my breath. I would fail a toxicity test right now because I can barely remember my own name, there's no way I could coordinate my limbs enough to walk in a straight line, and even attempting to recite the alphabet, either backward or forward would be nothing but unmitigated disaster.

When I feel the rasp of his tongue on my clit and the scratch of his five o'clock shadow against my inner thighs, I become completely incapable of controlling myself. I lower my knees and clasp my thighs tighter around his head, and somewhere in the back of my mind I hope it doesn't feel like he has his head in a vise.

They say that turnabout is fair play, and we're turned around. So, now it's my turn to make him lose his mind. I slick my tongue along the entire length of his cock, thrumming it against the ridges that swelled beneath my thumb a few minutes ago. It jerks in response, and he grunts. I envelop just the tip of it and hold it against the roof of my mouth, scraping it lightly against my molars.

He sucks the entire seam of me into his mouth and thrums his tongue against me the same way I just thrummed him. Apparently he thinks turnabout is fair play too. It's like he's plucking an invisible chord that starts at my center and creeps with agonizing slowness and heart-stopping surety all the way through the rest of my body, only escaping through my fingertips when I curl them into his thighs. "You taste like honey," he mutters.

The throb of his tenor against me now is more than an invisible chord.

It's the crescendo of an entire sonata, and I feel the tremors it ignites deep in my core. My legs quake and I'm suddenly having trouble holding myself upright.

I suck his entire length into my mouth, letting it hit the back of my throat. I work my jaws around his girth, and he growls when I somehow swirl my tongue down the sides. He swells even fuller, completely filling my mouth and throat. It's a fullness I welcome because it means he's at my mercy just as much as I'm at his. I'm ravaging him, reducing him to a creature of base need and I've never felt more powerful in my life.

"Just like that, please don't stop," he begs. And I feel the vibrations rumble against me like a wave pounding the shore, and then I'm drenching his tongue and he's burying his face even further into me, lapping up every last drop like it's the nectar of the gods.

His hands are on my hips, holding me in place. It's too much, and not enough.

I can't tell where I begin and end, where he begins and ends, we're just this straining, joined, wordless deluge of need. His hips thrust upward, a hard slash in the air, pressing against my sternum, and then I taste the salt of him in my mouth. I swallow it down like he's swallowing me.

It's the best sex I've ever had, and it's technically not even sex. I wonder if he feels the same way.

"Christ, you're magnificent," he murmurs into my skin.

Okay, so he does feel the same. That knowledge is a warm glow I can carry inside me along with the pleasure I just stole from him.

Chapter 21

Blake

SHE COLLAPSED AGAINST ME as soon as I pulled her into the circle of my arms. She was asleep within minutes, right after she gave me a peck on the cheek and told me that was the best sex she's ever had. Before I could correct her, she'd whispered that yes, she knew it technically wasn't sex. But she'd insisted it was still more and the best.

I agree. It was more and the best for me too. And I want her to tell me I belong to her. There must be something I can do to keep her from running away from me and from the way I'm making her feel. I want to tell her that I understand why she's scared. That I won't ever pressure her to go somewhere or do something that she doesn't feel comfortable doing. That I'll be there to rub her shoulders and hold her hand if she has a panic attack. That I'll be there to carry her away whenever she needs me to. No questions asked. And never ever any judgment.

We're spooning in the middle of my huge bed. She has her hands pressed together beneath her cheek and her face is still flushed. She tossed and turned a lot, until she finally kicked all the sheets and the cover to the bottom of the bed. She settled down after that, snuggling against me. She has an adorable little kerfluffle of a snore, and I could lay here forever watching her and listening to her. I press my hand against her chest every so often, to reassure myself she's still there and still breathing. That she isn't a product of my hyperactive imagination.

I'm plotting how I can keep her here even after her cabin is fixed when I hear the scratch of claws on the door.

Sasha probably needs to go out, and I'm not going to wake up the sated woman lying beside me. I pull on a pair of boxers and open the door. She makes no move to head outside. Instead, she nudges my hand with her cold nose and gives it a single, peremptory lick.

I think that means she finally accepts me. I push the door open wider and she saunters in, turning her entire body around in three counterclockwise circles before she settles down on the floor on my side of the bed. She's telling me she accepts me, and she's also letting me know that she'll guard us both. I hope she knows I'll guard the two of them as well.

Two weeks have passed, and we've been so busy, we've just slipped into this nightly ritual of sandwiches and cuddling on the couch to watch the Food Channel. We ride my bike to the school every morning and hold hands when we walk through the door. Each school day starts with me walking her to her room and dropping a kiss on her lips – like we're in middle school. We haven't discussed what happened between us, and even though I'm ready for a repeat the moment she requests it, I'm content with where we're now too. She sleeps curled against me every single night and we have deep discussions about things I've never talked about with anyone else.

She tells me about the parts of her squished down because her parents didn't approve of them. When she was twelve, she saved all her babysitting money so she could buy a magenta and hot pink scarf, mitten and knit cap set. Her mom told her she was making a spectacle of herself when she wore it. She said her mom's disapproval crushed her spirit, but she still defiantly wore it. Because it made her feel stronger than the weight of that disapproval. She wore it every day for two months straight. She was scared to wash it because she knew it would probably disappear and go the same place the funky socks she loved went. Banished to the charity clothing drive when her mom went through her closet and systematically got rid of everything with too much personality.

I'm sitting on the bleachers after the game when Seth Murray slides in beside me. He claps me on the back and chuckles. "We haven't had this much excitement since the music teacher ran away with the father of her show choir star."

I'm annoyed that the entire staff is speculating about my relationship with Sarah. She's so intensely private, I know she's probably eating lunch in her classroom and avoiding eye contact with everyone but me. "This is still really new,"

I correct. "We won't be running away together. I don't run from anything. I run toward it."

He throws his hands in the air. "No offense intended! We could all just tell things were moving a lot faster than we thought they would."

"It doesn't feel fast to me."

"Whatever, dude," he scoffs. "No guy in this town has even turned her head and now you come along with your tattoos and your motorcycle and your money and suddenly she's living with you. We're all wondering how you did it."

Now I'm angry. I'm angry that everyone feels entitled enough to reduce us to a cliché. I'm angry that it's probably making Sarah feel like something in a petri dish. "She's living with me because the derecho ripped off her roof," I tersely inform him.

"That can't be the whole story," he coaxes.

"That's all of it I'm going to share. We're both trying to make our lives here, and whether that's together or separately, that's no one's business but our own." There are a lot of things I love about living here, but the nosy meddling isn't one of them.

I've heard a lot of people say it's just because these communities care for each other, and it's an extension of that. A way to look out for everyone. Now that I'm in the middle of all the speculation I've seen aimed at others, it doesn't feel like anyone's being benevolent. It feels like they're trying to unearth deep, dark secrets so they can be self-righteous in the knowledge that they have the latest scoop. It has nothing to do with taking care of people, it has to do with people making themselves feel superior and adding to their social status as someone 'in the know'. It's not benevolent. It's petty and self-serving. At least in most cases.

"You do know there's a betting pool, right?" he interrupts my fixation on scowling into the distance.

"What?"

He obviously hears the menace in my question because he shrugs and throws his hands in the air again like it's something that can't be helped. "It's just something they do here," he informs me. As if that's an excuse. Doing something because they've always done it does not excuse their exploitative behavior.

"That's exploitation," I thunder. I'm disgusted.

"It's not meant to be. Taren and Zane didn't seem to mind," he defensively retorts.

"How do you know?" I bark. "Did anyone bother asking them how it felt to have everyone so invested in the outcome of their love story?"

"Not exactly," he admits.

"Please tell me you get how this is intrusive."

"I guess I can understand why you'd feel that way."

"Ms. Fraser is a very private person. I'm sure she doesn't welcome all this gossip. And neither do I. Life is too unpredictable as it is, and love too volatile, to have to deal with the weight of others' expectations."

"We're not expecting anything."

"Bullshit," I mutter. How did I fail to realize what an asshole this guy is? "The fact that a betting pool even exists means there are expectations."

"So what do you want me to do about it? I was just making conversation."

No, he was digging for insider information. But I don't bother correcting him. "If anyone says anything to you, just let them know how I feel. Let them know that the town benefactor doesn't appreciate his personal life being dragged through the mud puddles."

"Sure, I'll do my best," he laconically agrees. "But I hope you know you're fighting a losing battle."

He doesn't bother shaking my hand before he leaves. I'm sure I made my feelings crystal clear. He knows the last thing I want to do right now is shake it in return. I probably just cemented my reputation as a flaming asshole, but I don't give a shit. I know for a fact Sarah would be mortified if she knew we were the hot topic of conversation across every dinner table in town.

Chapter 22

Sarah

MY HEAD IS THROWN back so I can rinse the suds from my hair. It's hanging loose and wet around my shoulders. The shower is the only place I go without the armor of a braid, a bun, or a ponytail. My eyes are closed and I'm reliving the feel of his lips against my throat, and the way it felt to be caged against his wall of heat. My anxiety is swirling down the drain with every relentless drip of the water, and I'm relaxing for the first time in weeks. He has me tied up in knots and the constant tug of war between my fear and my feelings has imprinted on every single one of my tense, sore muscles. I'm leaning my head against the wall, blind and deaf to the world, just soaking up the way the water is pounding relief into my neck and shoulders.

I'm so lost in my thoughts; I barely register the dim splash. When I feel a light touch against my back I leap straight up and go sliding on the slick tiles. And crash right into him.

"I didn't mean to scare you."

"Well, you did," I bluster and cross my arms over my chest.

"Are you okay?" He's stripped of everything but a pair of black briefs. I know I can lie and tell him everything's fine. I doubt he'll believe me, but if I say it he'll take it as a cue to leave me alone. And I know he'll do it without hesitation. Even though it's his house. He said he won't press me for more than I'm ready to give. But every time I'm near him he wears down my resistance. I want to tell him everything.

I want to tell him about the whispers and the snickers in the hallway. About the way Principal Greene gave me a condescending look this morning when I turned in my roster and muttered, "Oh, how the mighty have fallen." I want to tell him about the glares that have been drilling holes in the back of my head every time I walk into the faculty breakroom.

"I thought you might be upset about the betting pool," he looks apologetic.

"If only that were all there is to be upset about," I mumble.

He steps into the shower with me and reels me into his arms. "This town is full of nosy assholes."

"The betting pool doesn't bother me so long as it's in good fun. But some people are being vindictive about it. Like I either fell off a pedestal they think I placed myself on or I snatched up the last eligible bachelor in three counties. It's making it really hard to take this one day at a time. I feel like I'm suddenly someone like the woman from that song *Harper Valley P.T.A.*," I confess.

He clenches his fists against my hips. "Has anyone been outright mean or said anything to your face?" He demands.

I know that if I tell him yes he will immediately take names, step out, and grind them to dust. "People have mostly muttered under their breath or just looked at me like I'm the evil queen that overthrew the kingdom."

"Why?" he asks, his brow furrowed in confusion. "You've never done anything to warrant their enmity."

"No, but I'm a come here, not a from here," I explain. "They think I haven't been here long enough to deserve you."

"What the hell does that even mean? Because you weren't born and raised here? Like a prime slab of grass-fed cow or something? That makes no sense. If that's what it means, you would deserve me because I'm not a from here either."

I can't help laughing. I should've known he would show me how ridiculous the whole situation is. "You're right," I lean my head against his chest. "Why do I let them get to me?"

"You shouldn't. There's a reason I'm standing in this shower with you. Even if you're not exactly all in."

I loop my arms around his neck. "And what reason is that?"

"Because you didn't chase me," he tweaks my nose between his thumb and forefinger. "I did all the chasing. I'm still doing the chasing."

"I don't like putting myself out there," I blush and smile into the crick of his neck. "I left all of that stuff behind me," I clarify.

"Then I should be extraordinarily grateful I'm the exception to your rule."

I nod my head against him. "Yes, you should."

He cages me loosely in his arms, nudging my chin up. "I can't believe you're here," he swallows thickly. "It took every ounce of my determination not to cross the line of trees that separated our yards and knock on your door and beg you to let me finish what we started against those lockers."

I can clearly see the outline of his erection, and I know he sees my gaze sweep over it. But he makes no move to adjust himself or hide it. "I might not have turned you away," I taunt. "But we'll never know, will we?"

"You're playing with fire, Fierce Girl. You do know that I have a bad boy reputation, right?"

"You keep saying that." I back away from him and recline against the wall just underneath the showerhead. The water cascades over me, and I watch him stalk forward until he's under it too.

"They say that bad boys can bring you heaven. Do you believe that?"

"Yes. But I also believe in reforming rakes. And you're not a bad boy, you're just a teddy bear in disguise," I place my hand on his chest. "And I'm not mad about it."

"A teddy bear? Really? Isn't that like a cinnamon roll?"

I'm surprised he's so well-versed in romance reader lingo. "Just how many romance books have you read since you went to the book club meeting?"

"A lot. I figured out that I have a lot of time on my hands to listen to audiobooks and the Libby app is amazing. I downloaded that pirate book yesterday," he wiggles his eyebrows at me. It's corny, but I love it.

"Did you really?" I squeal in excitement.

"I did. I thought maybe we could act out some of those scenes on the imaginary prow of my ship," he suggests hopefully.

"I would love that," I want to jump up and down, but I'm afraid I'll fall and end up yanking us both down.

"Give me some time to plan," he drops a kiss against my temple and reaches above me to turn the water off. "We stayed in here so long we ran out of hot water," he steps out and reaches for the big, fluffy towel that's been warming on the rack.

He holds it open for me when I step out, and then wraps me up like a pig in a blanket.

He didn't grab a towel for himself. My eyes are probably like giant flying saucers, mesmerized by that expanse of skin stretched over taut muscle.

His gaze darkens to burnished oak. "Do you want me to strut for you?"

"No. I don't know what I want." And I don't. I want him to leave me alone to wallow in self-pity. But I also want him to stay and make me forget about the world outside these walls.

"Well, I want to strut for you," he steps closer and puts his hands over mine where they're holding the towel closed. "I want to touch you. I want to give you pleasure with my hands and my mouth."

I gulp. I want that too. The last time I touched him, and he touched me, we got lost in it. We got lost in it and then became the latest topic of viral gossip. I can't help wanting it to happen again, even though I know there will be consequences. "Touch me where?"

"I want to nip at your bottom lip because it always looks like you've been biting it. I want to flick my thumbs over your lush, taut nipples. I want that fucking cross in my mouth. And the stud in your navel I didn't know was there until the other night. I want to stroke every inch of that tattoo on your lower back with my tongue, and bend you forward so I can slide my aching cock against you while you brace your hands on the wall. I want to skim your breasts with my teeth and suck them until you're on the verge of coming. Then I want to tug them into hard little points with my hands wrapped around them, while I let my mouth and tongue slide over your clit."

His words dance over my skin and wrap around me like a sirocco off the coast of the Mediterranean. I'm unfurling, like a night-blooming lily. Shy and trembling and eager and scared, seeking out the moonbeams.

I want all those things so ferociously it rattles in my chest. I want him with a ferocity that terrifies me. If I jump, will he catch me? Or will I fall into the canyon I fell in before and become nothing but brokenness scraped raw over a bundle of scars? If I take the risk, will I regret it? He says he's here to stay, but it's too hard for me to trust what people say. Especially men. Actions speak louder than words, and even though he claims he's walking the knife's edge of obsession, that can all be punctured and deflate in the space of a heartbeat. Because it seems too big to exist.

If I jump and there's an expiration date, will I be able to go on? Will I become a shell of who I am now and be forced to reinvent myself once again? Will I have to fit my jagged pieces between the four corners of a jigsaw puzzle I can't make sense of?

"Your thoughts are swirling in your eyes like pinwheels. What are they?" His tone is gentle, like he can feel me splintering apart in the breath of space between us.

"I know what I want, but I don't think it's wise to want it."

"What's so unwise about it?"

"The more I open up, the more power I give you. The more power I give you, the greater the chances that I'll lose myself."

"I won't let you lose yourself," he fiercely promises. "That would mean I was losing the woman I'm falling in love with."

I close my eyes at his admission. I let my lashes flutter against my cheeks, as he steps closer, and lifts my hands from the towel. Letting it crumple to the floor in a sodden heap. Lifting me into his arms and pressing my cheek against his chest. I snuggle against him, letting the tears leak from the corners of my eyes. He sits down on the edge of the bed with me cradled in his embrace. His thumb sweeps across my cheek, lifting it to his mouth and licking away the sorrow he brushed away.

"I don't know why I'm crying," I gurgle into his armpit.

"You're crying because your heart is hurt. You don't understand petty cruelty or jealousy because it's something you'd never indulge in."

"You have a skewed vision of me," I mumble. "I get jealous."

"I'm sure you do, Fierce One, but you don't get vindictive. I doubt you have a single vindictive bone in your whole body," he responds confidently.

"It's still no reason for me to cry."

"It is. I may not know much, but I know you came to Willow Creek for sanctuary, and you feel betrayed. That's why you're crying." He lifts my face away from his shoulder and tips my chin up, forcing me to meet his gaze. "You're giving them too much power with your tears. People who have emptiness inside them are always trying to burst the happiness of others. There are still a lot of people in this town who value you and will stand behind you. Don't let the bad eggs ruin your experience or your perceptions."

"It's hard. Sometimes those voices are the loudest."

"I won't let them be. I'll tell you everything you need to hear seventy-five thousand times a day or more. Whenever you need to hear it."

He's so confident we're moving toward a destination that will always include him. The closer we become, the less far-fetched it seems. The issue is that it's hard for me to put my trust in something that still seems surreal.

The next day passes in a blur. We won again, and I'm over the moon. We only need to win two more games to guarantee our berth in the playoffs and there's no way that's not going to happen. We've already defeated the teams with the rankings closest to ours. It's one of the only nights the boys' and girls' teams don't both have games. Blake was here for most of it, but he let me know at break that he didn't want to miss his weekly call with Ellery. I promised to fill him in on the final outcome.

I hear him laughing when I kick off my shoes at the door. I grab the plate with grilled cheese he set out on the counter for me and a big glass of milk and creep into the living room. His eyes are closed, and his laughter is slowly melting away. I step on one of the creaking floorboards and he pins me with his gaze. "Come here, Sarah. It's time you met the other woman in my life."

"Ooh yes!" A woman squeals. "I want to see the woman who's helping me make my big brother nothing but a pile of mush."

I cautiously approach. The laptop is balanced on his knees and Woodrow is propped on a cushion beside him. He's wearing a little red cloak and a hat with a pair of tiny horns. This must be the latest of Ellery's gifts. Sasha is sprawled on the rug beside the coffee table, snoring lightly.

When I settle into the couch on his other side, he throws an arm around me to pull me closer, so the camera can capture us both. A young woman with a pixie cut and ears studded with earrings looks back at me. Her eyes are darker than Blake's, more walnut than cherry. "Hi Sarah!" She gushes enthusiastically. "It's so great to meet you! Zane's told me so much, I feel like I already know you. I can't believe you convinced him to start reading romance!"

I laugh despite my nervousness. I feel like we just stepped across some invisible relationship threshold. I haven't even told him about my family, let alone introduced him. It would be nowhere near as delightful as this meeting. "It didn't take much convincing," I confide. "I think he was looking for inspiration on how to lure me into his bed and thought it was a sure path."

Her whole face lights up. "He left out that part of the story. I hope you're playing hard to get. Women have made it too easy for him."

"I like to keep him guessing where he stands," I blushingly reply.

"That's an excellent strategy!" Ellery claps her hands together, applauding me.

"How's your dissertation going?"

She launches into a discussion about all the challenges she's facing because one of here theorems was transposed by the lab assistant and she didn't realize the mistake until yesterday. She's brilliant and I can't wait to read her paper. "Blake's eyes are glazed over and he looks like he needs a nap," she laughs. "We'd better wrap up."

"I'd love to read your final paper."

"Of course! I'll bring it to Thanksgiving. Blake said Taren and Zane invited everyone to a Friendsgiving Dinner at the farmhouse. I can't wait to meet everyone!"

"You're going to charm them just like you do everyone, Pipsqueak," Blake affectionately responds.

"Goodbye, Sarah! I'm so glad I finally got to meet you," she replies, and then turns to her brother. "Don't chase this one away with your alpha hole alter ego," she warns. "Love you, Big Bro."

After she signs off, we snuggle on the couch, rewatching season one of Ted Lasso. Blake insisted we do that before we start watching season two. My legs are stretched across his lap and he's massaging the balls of my feet, and then I'm waking up curled against his chest as he carries me up the stairs to the bedroom. "I can walk," I protest.

"Nope. You're sleeping in my bed tonight."

I don't protest again. When I sleep with his arms around me, the nightmares stay away.

Emma sent me a frantic text this morning. She said some guy in a black Cadillac rolled into town looking for me. He saw the crowded café and figured that was as good a place to start his search as any. So he started asking questions. And of course the town busybodies were easily charmed and more than happy to share the latest gossip about the former soccer star science teacher and her budding romance with the hot developer.

Emma said he looked like he'd eaten a whole bucket of lemons by the time they were finished regaling him with their story. She said she knows she's seen his face before, but she can't remember where.

She's seen him alright. Most of America has. Edgar Percival Vandervilt the Third made headlines last year when he decided to throw his bid into the ring for POTUS. He got shut out early on after a dismal showing at the Iowa caucus, but his impeccably groomed appearance and rugged good lucks garnered national attention.

He loves to talk about his time in the firehouse – which he spent ordering everyone else around according to one of my childhood friends. He loves to talk about his entrepreneurship – which has always been funded by his senator father's deep pockets and ended in disaster. He loves to talk about the one woman who got away – and how he hasn't stopped looking for her.

That woman is me and I didn't want to be found.

I don't know how he found me. He's the last person I expected to waltz into Cupcake on Main. I haven't talked to him since the morning I climbed out the window and snuck away like a burglar leaving the scene of a crime. I don't know what the fall-out was from my disappearing act.

I just know I left for a reason. I looked in that mirror and I didn't recognize the woman I'd become. I didn't want to be her. I didn't want to be known as a gracious hostess and someone you can always count on to carry the conversation. I didn't want to be known as the politician's wife in training, trotted out on the campaign trail to earn the family vote.

When Beth died, he ostensibly stepped in to comfort me. That's what it looked like on the surface. To an outside observer he was everything solicitous and sympathetic. All of that is feigned. He will steamroll over anyone that gets in his way, and either leave them lying in the dirt or guilt them into becoming a version of themselves he can use to his advantage. He thought my social anxiety was a weakness. He thought the best way to fix it was to pretend it didn't exist, to shove it under the rug and shame me into feeling like my aversion to confrontation was why my sister died.

It's taken four years of therapy to begin untangling the mess he made. I only gave him a year of my life and when I look back on it, I don't even recognize the person he molded me into.

Blake's former level of douchebaggery doesn't even touch the levels my former fiancé will sink to. No one fits that definition better than him. No one uses people like him. He brags about his connection to Cornelius Vanderbilt and calls him "my railroad baron great-great-great uncle." It's a point of pride to him that his ability to squash everyone else on his way up seems to be an inherent genetic trait. He purposefully ignores the "robber baron" reputation of said ancestor. A man notorious for exploitation, bribery and steamrolling his competition. Capitalism at its horridly oppressive best.

Now it's confrontation time. I'm not mentally prepared, but I don't have a choice.

I throw my shoulders back and push open the door. He strides toward me, smiling superciliously while his assistant starts snapping pictures with his phone. He holds his arms out to me and I stay right where I'm standing. There's a flash of annoyance and then he walks closer, making an attempt to grab my hands in his. I keep my arms crossed over my chest and glower.

"I've thought about you every day for the last five years, Sarah."

"Well I stopped thinking about you a long time ago. Except in terms of the damage I know you're capable of."

"Why are you here, Sarah? You're a woman who glitters, not one that hides. You're Helen, not Cassandra. What are you doing teaching biology to a bunch of high school students who will never appreciate you?"

"What am I doing?" I grit my teeth. I drop my arms to my sides and clench my knuckles into fists and dig my nails into my palms to keep from exploding. To prevent myself from strangling him. "What am I doing? I'm doing something I should've done long before I climbed out that window," I say fiercely.

"And what is that? Running away?"

"No. Not running away. Running toward. I'm becoming a woman who stands on her own two feet and doesn't let other people tell her what and who she needs to be. A woman who would never have been possible if she'd stayed in Ada, Washington because every last detail of her life was scripted and choreographed."

"You're fooling yourself of you think the simple life is for you. Your parents are Nobel Prize winners for chrissake," he scoffs. "You're deluding yourself if you think you'll ever be happy with mediocrity."

"This isn't mediocrity."

"Hear, hear," mutters one of the customers. All the hubbub around us has died because everyone is straining to catch every last word of this interaction. Hopefully they won't take it to the tabloids. I don't feel like having my face plastered all over the National Enquirer.

"It is mediocrity. You'll never convince me otherwise. It took the private investigator I finally hired more than six months to track you down. Let's face the music. You'll never be happy here. And you don't have to be. You can be happy with me," he moves toward me again and I step backward. "I'm prepared to forgive you for leaving me at the altar," someone gasps at this revelation. "I'm prepared to take you back home where you belong."

I can't stand his condescension. I can't believe I was ever fooled into believing his contrition. "I'm not a child. My decision to leave you standing there wasn't an arbitrary one. You're a marionette, your strings pulled by your father the senator and your mother the judge. You don't love me. You love the thought of me, and the thought of my family's prestige adding to your own reputation. I was carefully culled from the herd for the sake of my gene pool and my connections."

"Well, your parents don't think so. We all want what's best for you. What's keeping you here, Sarah?"

Chapter 23

Blake

I CAN'T HEAR THEIR conversation. But I can see the woman I'm falling in love with. She looks like she's holding her ground, but she looks defeated too. Like she's resigning herself to some inevitable outcome. I can tell this asshole, whoever he is, is trying to pressure her into something she wants nothing to do with. He keeps creeping closer, until he's in her space, looming over her like one of the gargoyles on the roof of the Notre Dame.

Emma's text was terse. *You need to swing by Cupcake on Main ASAP.*

I left my socket wrench lying on the floor of the garage and decided the work I needed to do on my car could wait. I didn't even know she had my number. Which immediately told me these were dire circumstances. She looks frantic, because the attention of every single booth is hard-wired to the drama playing out in front of them.

I can feel Sarah's anxiety spiraling as if it was my own. I'm willing to bet this asshole knows exactly how he's making her feel and doesn't care, because he thinks her reaction to their public conflict makes her more susceptible to his manipulation. He's obviously someone she ran away from. Which means she needs rescued. Whether she wants it or not.

I let the door swing open so hard it bangs against the wall. Everyone's gaze snaps to me. Emma glares at me, and then shakes her head, smirking. She knows I was making a statement with my dramatic entry.

I didn't bother cleaning up. I have grease on my hands, grease streaks on my jeans, and probably grease on my face. I threw on my leather jacket over a sleeveless t-shirt that has a candy skull graphic, and I have on a beat-up pair of vintage motorcycle boots. The asshole who's trying to simultaneously berate and coax Sarah skims his gaze over me, curls his lip in derision, and then turns away. Ignoring me. Putting me in a little box called "beneath my notice."

I don't look like the kind of guy who has a stake in this. At least compared to him. He's polished and slick, like a Hugo Boss ad. I stride toward them anyway, and casually slip my arm around Sarah's waist. I feel her tense beneath my touch, but she doesn't jerk away. Instead, she moves closer. Okay. She's telling me without telling me that she needs my support. That she doesn't want whatever this dude is trying to sell.

"Who are you?" I interrupt, drawling out the question because I sense it will annoy him.

"That's none of your business," his voice is prissy and stuck-up, and I can tell he's annoyed. Yay. Mission accomplished.

"Why's it none of my business?" I prod, interrupting him again.

"Because this is my former fiancée. If you want to get technical, she's still my fiancée because she left the ring on the vanity, snuck out a window and threw her dress in a dumpster. She never officially called it off."

"I'd say that throwing her dress in a dumpster was a good indication of how much she wanted to marry you," I observe. I lean closer. "Which obviously wasn't as badly as you thought," I dramatically whisper.

A couple of the avid watchers chuckle behind their hands.

"Yeah, dude. I think if she was serious she would've kept the ring," barks one.

We've never been introduced, but I think it's the old guy who owns the hardware store. He's not lying. "Why are you here?" I pointedly ask this guy who obviously doesn't belong in Willow Creek.

"I'm here for the woman I love," he imperiously informs me.

"No, you're not," I scoff. "You're here because she hurt your pride and now you're questioning whether you have some fatal flaw. You're here for justification, not for love. Even I can see that, and we haven't even been formally introduced."

Sarah's been quiet during this whole exchange. But she hasn't refuted anything I've said. Instead, she's standing resolutely by my side.

"Allow me to remedy that," he says officiously. "I am Edmund Percival Vandervilt the Third. I represent Washington's District 6 in the House of Representatives."

I want to rub my hands together like Stripe from the Gremlins. "That explains so much."

"Like what?" he suspiciously asks.

"Like why you look like a fish out of water. Like why you're trying to convince this woman to listen to your pathetic excuses and follow you back to wherever you came from."

"How's that?"

"Because she's probably the only real thing you've ever known. And you know you can leverage that into your political image. She's just a prop to you," I'm furious. "She deserves to be more than a facsimile of herself. She deserves the chance to become someone she's comfortable seeing in the mirror. She deserves the chance to stand on her own two feet. I won't let you make her feel less for wanting those things. I won't let you take them away from her."

"Blake, he knows I'm not leaving," Sarah places her hand on my arm.

"Does he, Fierce Girl? I don't think so. He wouldn't still be standing here, trying to persuade you."

"I don't need you to fight my battles for me," she pleads.

"I'm here whether or not you need me," I brush a curl off her cheek.

"While I find this maudlin exchange fascinating, she still hasn't answered my question," interrupts Edgar the Douchebag.

"What question is that?"

"What's keeping her here. She hasn't really answered my question. Her meager explanation won't satisfy her parents and it certainly doesn't satisfy me."

"Why should I care that it doesn't satisfy you, Ed?"

"I told you not to call me by that ridiculous nickname," he glares at her. "You should care because I can make your life very uncomfortable. I have no problem going to the tabloids and throwing your past in your face. I have no problem making this town a three-ring circus," he threatens.

She visibly gulps. And I feel her entire body seize in denial. I want to intervene, but this guy won't take her seriously if I do. He still might not take her seriously and, if he doesn't, then I'll resolve the issue with my fists. But first I need to let her put him in his place.

"I'm not going to let you blackmail me," she states with quiet dignity.

"You won't have a choice. I know what makes you tick, and I know how to exploit your weaknesses. I'm not above doing that to get what I want."

"Let me know when I have your permission to hit him," I mumble. Not loud enough for him to hear, but loud enough to let her know I'm not going to stand idly by and listen to him threaten her for an indefinite period of time. Letting her know I'm barely holding my temper in check.

She squeezes my arm to stall me and shakes her head imperceptibly. She's telling me to restrain myself just a little longer.

"I'm not above doing what I have to in order to get what I want either," she informs him. And the Ice Queen is back. Her voice is pure winter, and she could freeze him where he stands if she wanted to.

He laughs derisively. The sound echoes in the crowded café. I decide I've had enough. I step forward, brushing away Sarah's cautionary hand on my arm. "What are you laughing at?" I snarl.

"I'm laughing at how pathetic this is. She'll cave like she always does because she's deficient. She can't even function in public. She needs me and she needs her parents because we're her crutches."

"No you're not. Not anymore," my arm snaps toward him and I plow my fist into his face. I hope I'm permanently rearranging it. He rears back, his nose streaming blood.

"You fucking caveman!" he screams hysterically, "You probably broke my nose and I have a press conference tomorrow!"

"Good. You can tell them you got it honestly. You can tell them you got it because you were trying to intimidate and manipulate someone you perceived as weaker than you and someone stepped in to correct your assumptions."

"I'll sue you, you fucking grease monkey!" he yells.

I shrug. "Sue me. You won't like the publicity. And I have the resources to uncover all your dirty secrets. The tabloids will think Christmas came early this year."

"You're just some local guy she's banging. It'll never go anywhere. She's a frigid bitch who's completely incapable of functioning like a normal person in social situations."

My fist makes contact with his temple this time. He falls to the floor like a toppling Jenga tower. Knocked out cold. My brawling skills must not be as rusty as I thought. The whole café erupts into cheers.

"Should you have done that?" Sarah asks quietly.

"Yes. He didn't know when to shut up."

"He might press charges," she says worriedly, biting her lip.

"I'll tell him to bring it on. If he does that he's just challenging me to dig up every single one of his skeletons."

"He has let some things slip; I know he's not as squeaky clean as he wants everyone to think he is."

"Yeah, I didn't figure he was. He's too pretentious and self-righteous. I'm not worried about him." These guys are all the same. Throwing their imaginary weight around and leaning hard on their precious family legacies because they don't have the guts to sever the apron strings. They usually have really disgusting skeletons hiding in their closets because they think they won't get caught because they're above the law. I'll drag all his sordid secrets into the burning daylight in a heartbeat if he presses me to.

"Maybe we need to chill for a while," she interrupts my thoughts.

"Why? We're not hurting anyone." I don't want her to run away from us. If she runs away now, at the first sign of an obstacle, how hard is she going to fight when there's way more at stake? I grab her hands. "Please don't turn me away," I plead.

She jerks her hands out of my grasp and starts wringing them. "I'm worried, Blake."

I know she's worried because she's calling me Blake instead of Shark. "Why are you worried? I told you I wasn't."

"If he's here, that means my parents aren't that far behind. That means that the shooting will get dragged into the news again, because they'll all use it to pressure me into moving back to Washington. I can't afford to give them any more ammunition."

"Since when did I become ammunition?"

"You were always potential ammunition. I mean look at us…" she waves her hands between us as if that's supposed to enlighten me.

"What do you mean, look at us?" I try, and fail, to keep my question from coming out harsh and confrontational.

"You're the rebel and I'm the good girl," she elaborates.

"On what planet are you the good girl? You wear that mask, and everyone thinks you're the good girl. But you have tattoos and a nipple piercing. You're a rebel in your heart – that's why you're attracted to me. You can be yourself with me." I step forward and she backs up.

"Maybe that's not who I need to be," she sighs. "We've had fun, but I think we need to chill for a while. My house will be done by Wednesday. I can stay with Emma until then."

"So you're pushing me away?"

"No. We can still be friends," she holds a hand out for me to shake.

This is what she wants to reduce us to. Friends who shake hands. I know I said I would wait forever, but everything inside me is cracking open right now. I don't know how she's able to walk away like we're not building something.

"Fine," I mutter resignedly. "I'll help you move your things out."

"You don't need to. I'll let Emma know I want to move in tonight. I only have the suitcase and Sasha. I'll just drive my truck over there. She has plenty of designated on-street parking."

"Don't hold back," I say grimly.

"The sooner I'm out of your way, the better."

"You're not in my way. But you're determined to act like a wrecking ball, and I know I won't be able to change your mind."

I don't get drunk very often. When I do, it's rarely on purpose. Tonight, I'm getting drunk on purpose. The house is dark, and it feels empty without her here. I'm nursing a bottle of Wild Turkey Rare Breed when someone pounds on my door.

I stumble to the door, tripping over the ottoman and stubbing my toe. I'm cursing at the pain and hopping up and down when I yank the heavy wood open. I half-heartedly believed it was her, having second thoughts and ready to tell me I could ignore everything she said today.

It's not. It's Zane and Dex. Zane's arms are loaded with brown bags that look like they came from the liquor store. Dex is carrying a casserole bag.

Zane taps me in the chest and pushes me back. "We came to your rescue as soon as we heard."

"There's nothing you can do to help," I protest.

"Dude, that's bullshit. We can commiserate with you. I've been where you are. It's called the third act break-up. And Dex knows he'll have to eventually muddle his way through one too. Think of this as a learning experience for him and an *it's always darkest before the dawn* moment for you. You owe it to yourself and him to wallow in front of your friends."

"Misery doesn't always love company," I mutter.

"We're here to lift you out of your misery. We're going to help you fix things. We brought more liquor and Dex made better than sex dip for the nachos I know you have in your pantry."

I let them push their way inside. Zane puts his hands in his hips and looks around, shaking his head. "I thought she left this afternoon?"

"She did," I rub my hands over my face.

"Then why does it look like a herd of wild pigs ransacked your living room?"

I shrug. "I've been wallowing. And I felt like throwing things earlier."

"Hunh," he grunts. And then he starts tidying up.

Chapter 24

Sarah

"You know I'm one of your best friends," is how Emma begins the conversation. "And I need to say this not just because I want to win the betting pool, but because I've never seen you happier than you are with him."

"Just say it," I'm curled up on her couch, eyes closed, my head resting against the cushions.

"You're being an idiot."

That makes me open my eyes. I glare at her. "How am I being an idiot?"

"Obviously, you didn't want to break up with him. What are you doing?"

"I'm trying to get my head on straight. If I'm going to fend off my overbearing ex and whatever reinforcements he brought, and whatever shitstorm he's planning to rain down on my head, I don't need distractions."

"This man basically told you he thinks you're his future. How's that a distraction?"

"I need to focus on keeping my head down instead of dragging all of us through the mud."

She throws her hands up in exasperation. "Since when did you become responsible for everyone else?"

"It's my fault he's here. If he hadn't been looking for me, no one else would've been dragged into the spotlight," I explain.

"Let's be clear about something," she stalks forward and sinks into the cushions across from me. "I can take care of myself. So can the rest of us. We're not going to let some pretentious asshole jerk us around."

"You guys have no idea what kind of power he wields."

"And he has no idea who he's dealing with. Do you think Blake and Zane don't have connections?"

I shrug my shoulders.

"Well they do. And I bet they have more pull than the strings this guy thinks he can yank on. I have them too. I don't want to open that door again, but I will do it to protect my friends. We're here for you. We don't blame you for any of this and we've got your back."

"It's my responsibility."

"No the hell it's not! Your only responsibility is to yourself. That means that you need to stop denying yourself. That man is halfway in love and you just sent him away like a dog who failed obedience school."

"My life is complicated. He came to Willow Creek to get away from complicated."

She rolls her eyes. "Please. Life is complicated. Anyone who thinks otherwise needs their head examined. Life can be painful and brutal. But it can also be full of joy and people who matter. This guy obviously matters to you. Stop acting like he doesn't."

"I never said he doesn't matter. It's just not the right time or place."

"You don't get to make that decision for him. He wants to fight for you. Give him the chance to do it." She fiercely admonishes. "I wish I had a guy willing to fight for me. I wish I had a guy who had no reservations about hitting the douchebags in my life."

"Taren still thinks you're a big part of the reason Trevor left. Because you acted like you were oblivious to him. Like he wasn't worth your time and if he made a move you'd attack him like a T-rex."

"We're not discussing me. And I think Taren's hallucinating."

"But didn't you say he dragged you under the mistletoe at the barn dance last year?" I prod. She never shared more details than that. I'm curious about what happened between them, but I'm also trying to distract her from lecturing me.

"Yes, he did. End of story. It was like oil and water."

"Hunh," I respond. Her cheeks are flushed bright pink and I don't believe her. "You still haven't told me why you stood me up. When it was your idea to participate in that stupid race in the first place."

"Well we might not be sitting here debating the merits of the hot new guy in town if I hadn't stood you up. You could show a little gratitude," she huffs and ignores my question.

"I think he would've found a way to weasel his way into my life, regardless. Taren said Zane told her he was snooping before we were even introduced."

"Point proven. He's definitely half in love with you and has been for some time. And you're kicking him to the curb just like that because you're scared."

"I'm not scared. Not exactly," I try to marshal my thoughts into some semblance of order. "I've just been down this road before, and I want to get out before there's a head-on collision and no way to avoid the wreckage."

"How is rolling over without even standing up for what you want the best decision? Just because the world has shaken your faith and broken you before, that doesn't mean you shouldn't take a chance on a different outcome. This is all part of your second chance. The final step in your journey. You can finally embrace the things that make you different from your obviously shitty parents and make your life here. You can make it very clear that this is what you choose. That you're not running away – you're running toward."

Her words remind me of something Blake said. "That's what he said he was doing."

"What further proof do you need that you two are meant for each other?"

"It just feels like we were moving too fast. That we were thrown together by hormones and circumstance."

"Just take it one day at a time. But give it a chance," she begs. "Please, Sarah. You deserve it and I want to see you claim the happiness you deserve," she leans forward and envelops me in a hug. I bury my nose in the cloud of her curls.

"What if I can't make myself take that step?" I mumble.

"I have faith in you. You never shied away from anything on the soccer field. Why would you shy away from this?"

Chapter 25

Blake

Zane and Dex convinced me to give her a week to make the next move. If that week goes by and she hasn't done anything to salvage what we have, then I'm going to fight for it. I'm even thinking about staging a Heath Ledger moment in the bleachers after one of her games.

The girls' team is number one in our division. I'm not surprised. The players are talented, but it's more than that. She coaches them to work together as a unit. That's why they're winning. Because they don't try to outshine each other. I'm still trying to get the guys on my team to incorporate that dynamic.

I'm not above plying my crochet needle either. I picked up chenille yarn in town the other day, and I'm going to sit in front of the tv tonight and start my next project.

I'm watching Season 2 of Ted Lasso, on the third row of stitches, when there's a tentative knock on my door. Heart in my throat, or maybe in the soles of my feet, I open the door.

It's her. Her hands are clasped tightly in front of her. The intoxicating scent of night jasmine, with hints of bourbon envelops me. She's in a stretched out ribbed tank that's seen better days, the periwinkle blue faded to a dingy gray. A pair of battered jeans shields her long legs from view.

"Do you want to help me find some nightcrawlers?" She tentatively asks. She's hovering in the doorway, half cloaked in shadow.

"Why?" I'm too scared of being burned to jump in feet first. I need to know why she's here.

"I want to go fishing again," she explains. "I always do it the weekend before a Wednesday game."

"That doesn't answer my question," I remonstrate. "You're perfectly capable of catching nightcrawlers by yourself. Why do you need me to go with you?"

She hesitates. "I don't exactly need you. I just wanted you."

So she doesn't need me, she wants me. That's an explanation I can work with. She's not severing my hamstrings or throwing me to the piranhas. "Okay," I acquiesce.

I slide on my shoes, grab the flashlight from her hand and lead her toward the pier. There's a half moon tonight, so we need the beam of the LED to carve a path into the semi-darkness. Did she really show up at my door because she wanted me to go hunt night crawlers? Or was that just an excuse?

She doesn't even have a bucket. I think she was just throwing reasons out there, trying to come up with some viable reason for a walk. Maybe the pier isn't the place I should be leading her if she has other things on her mind.

Maybe I need to find out what brought her to my door this late. I tug her up against a tree.

I can see the barest outline of her face. She gasps when I push her up against the rough bark, but I don't think it's because I'm hurting her. I can hear how fast she's breathing. I think she's forgotten what my touch feels like against her skin. I want to remind her. I bind her wrists in one hand and use my other one to rip her tanktop. The flimsy material has been washed so many times, it tears easily. She's not wearing anything underneath it. The cold gleam of that cross taunts me, flickering in the dim light.

I dip my head to slide my nose down the side of her neck. I make the caress languorous and tempting. I inhale her scent of tart cherry and honeyed bourbon, and feather light kisses along the arch of her jaw from just below her earlobe. She unconsciously eases her body further into my grip, angling her hips toward me like she's seeking relief from the torment.

I nip the pulse fluttering in the corded muscles of her throat, clenching it gently between my teeth. I can feel the hardened points of her nipples against my t-shirt, and I know she's aroused by the cold mist seeping off the water and the feel of my hands and mouth against her skin. I twist one of them, not quite a pinch between my thumb and forefinger, but enough to make her whimper in my arms. I tug it more firmly and bend close again to taunt her.

"You want me to fuck you, don't you?" I growl.

She doesn't answer, just looks up at me with stars reflected in her eyes, a siren call that is soft and warm and beckoning. If she doesn't answer me, doesn't assert herself, she can claim later that she was swayed against her better judgment. Hell no. If she wants me to touch her she has to accept the consequences of that touch – the burden of what it means and what it will cost us both.

She's a lightning rod in my hands, calling down the storm that's been crashing around in me since the first moment I saw her. She has to tell me that she wants this as much as I do. That no matter how many lies she tells herself she can't deny this, and she can't stay away.

"Answer me," I demand.

She closes her eyes, trying to get a grip on her emotions. "Yes," she whispers.

I drag the torn shirt slowly over each arm, brushing the tender skin on the inside of her upper arms, trailing across her elbows, drifting across each fingertip. Her eyes are still closed, and I lean forward, dropping butterfly kisses on her fluttering lashes and at the corners of each brow.

My forehead rests against hers and our breaths are staccato in the evening murmur of the woods. We sway irrevocably toward each other, suspended in a single moment that is a promise stretching between us.

She moves infinitesimally, a bare lift of her chin. But it's enough for her lips to touch mine. This is her yes and I'm taking it. We kiss like we're gangly, awkward fourteen-year-olds, mouths sealed and then hovering, a sweet temptation and a dare to be reckless.

A lion that's grown tired of batting around its prey, I swoop down on her. My lips touch every corner of hers, nipping them in the lightest of reprimands. My teeth graze the bottom curve of her soft, half-open lips. She sighs and shifts against me, her teeth clashing against my own and then sliding against my chin. She sticks her tongue in my dimple and lingers there for an endless second. "I wondered what you would taste like there," she softly confesses.

My hands burrow into her hair, loosening her ponytail so it spills over her shoulders and down her body. It's silver in the greenish-gray light of the half-darkened forest. I pick up the end of a curl that's flowing over her breast and stroke it across the hardened point of one nipple. She angles her body more deeply into the caress. I push her more firmly against the tree, wedging my thigh between her legs, so I'm clasped against her. I drop her hair and tilt her head back.

"I like having you at my mercy," my admission rumbles against the satin skin between her collarbones.

"Am I at your mercy? I think we're at each other's mercy," she contradicts me, sliding her hands across my biceps and then tangling them in my hair. "I think we've been at each other's mercy since we ended up on the ground after that race."

I've definitely been at her mercy since then. Caught up in a lethal fascination that makes me want things I never have.

Chapter 26

Sarah

I'VE BEEN CRAVING HIS touch for so long. I demolished the battery on my favorite vibrator because it's the one closest to his length and girth. I've been dreaming of what he'd feel like inside me, how my whole body would shiver and clench and quaver around him, how he'd move the bed with the power of his thrusts.

The muscles in his upper arms are tense because he's holding back. I don't want him to hold back. Even though I can feel the rough surface behind me, even though we're not in the most ideal location for finally giving in, none of it matters. I want to feel his bare skin against mine – the scrape of my breasts against the light dusting of hair on his chest, the glide of his iron thigh between my legs.

I bunch my hands in his t-shirt and yank it up his back, across the crests of those wide shoulders, and over his head. I push him away, just slightly. His fists are in his hips, his jeans slung low. I reach out and pull down the zipper, pushing the sides just under his navel. He's carved from marble, standing there, the outline of that deep vee of muscle etched just above his hip bones glimmering in the dim moonlight filtering through the canopy above us.

His eyes never leave mine as he pushes his jeans completely off. He's commando, and the cock I had my lips wrapped around just a few days before bobs between us. He edges closer again, and I retreat, my back thumping against the solidity of the tree behind me. It's a crutch against his relentless determination to ravage me. It's a crutch against the way he makes me long for things that have always been just beyond my reach.

His hands move to my jeans, and he flips open the button. He drags the zipper slowly down, grazing me with his knuckles. He pulls them down my legs, lifting them one at a time so he can ease them over my calves and ankles. He tosses them behind him, and they land across a bush. I went commando too. I didn't plan this, but I hoped for it. So now we're both standing here naked, our skin not the only way we've made ourselves vulnerable to each other. Our skin not the only thing bared between us.

"Someday you're going to tell me why you almost married someone like that. Why you ever thought that was all you deserved," he promises.

"I'm not the person I was then, not really. There are parts of her still inside me, still scared to take chances. But I want to take a chance with you. I want those parts of me banished to the corners," I can feel the sheen in my eyes, the seep of tears leaking down my cheekbones.

He catches one on the tip of his finger and lifts it to his mouth. "I will swallow your tears for you. I will be strong for your brokenness, my arms a place for you to shatter and heal. You can break on me. That's what I want to be for you."

The feelings inside me creep up my throat, closing it off. I'm incapable of speaking now, so I just nod my head in assent.

His hands bracket my face, and his lips are on mine again. This time I'm slowly drowning. I can see the buoy on the horizon behind me as I swim away from it. Chasing the waves that are slamming toward the shore with a single-minded determination to ignore the safety I've clung to for so long.

He slides a knuckle over my clitoris, then through my wetness. His teeth graze the pulse in my throat again, clenching there because he's staking his claim. "Did you make yourself come thinking about me?" he murmurs into my ear.

I shakily nod.

"Next time, I'm watching," he growls as he sinks two fingers into me. His thumb circles my clitoris as his index and forefinger twist inside me and it's almost too much to bear. My legs tremble and my whole body is a pliant strand of spaghetti, wilting beneath the competency of his hands. He strokes his fingers in and out, and I feel the jangle and thrum sizzle down every single one of my nerve endings.

He nips my earlobe and rubs my nipple with his other hand. He grasps it so tightly; I can feel the slight sandpaper of his callouses like a brand. It's a hard, sweet burn. I'm on the verge of losing myself in an orgasm when his fingers slow their torment.

"I need to get the condom from the back pocket of my jeans," he mutters. "But I don't want to stop touching you."

"I don't want you to stop touching me, but we need that condom. I'm tired of wondering what you'll feel like inside me…"

He groans, and steps slowly, reluctantly away. I watch him crouch down, completely entranced by the flex of his thighs and ass. Faster than I can blink, he's rummaged in his discarded clothes and is flourishing the condom. Eyes on me, he rips open the corner with his teeth and tears it open.

I move to touch him, but he bats my hands away. "Un unh," he shakes his head at me. "I want you to watch and imagine how you'll feel in a few minutes."

I dutifully watch. I want to tell him that the only reason I'm the picture of obedience is because I don't want to disrupt the moment. He slides the condom on with agonizing, excruciating, languor. His eyes on me the entire time. I drop my hand and tease my opening in front of him. Gathering my wetness and slicking it across my clitoris. He's swells even more, giving himself a hard tug while he stares at me, mesmerized.

I widen my stance and throw my shoulders back. Suddenly, he's there. "Arms around my neck," he commands. I oblige, and he crosses his forearms against my back to protect it from the tree. "Now I want you to lift your left leg and curl it around my waist. Then I want you to grab your ankle, so I know you're not going anywhere."

There's still a little niggle of rebellion, but I do it because I don't want to go anywhere. He slides into me with a groan that comes from his diaphragm. I feel the echoes of it against every inch of my skin. This angle makes me feel raw and exposed, and my fingers have a tenuous grip. He slams into me again, bracing me against his arms for protection, twisting his hips on the way back out so his thick head notches up against my clitoris, grazing it.

"Fucking wanted this for months," he hoists me higher, until my right foot is like a ballerina's en pointe, just my tip toes sweeping the ground.

The feel of him inside me is overwhelming. He bottoms out deep and hard, and I crumble. The way I clench him as I disintegrate makes him throw his head back. And then I feel him shake, and his whole body jerks in response. He drops his head against my shoulder, his sweat dripping down my clavicle. "Wanted to torture you more," he mutters.

"You've tortured me quite enough. You don't know how many times I've had to replenish my batteries," I giggle into the damp curls just behind his ear. He pulses inside me again. "Like that image do you?" I tease.

"Fierce Girl, you have no idea," he raises his head and his gaze locks on my upturned face. "I'll demonstrate again very soon."

He leans away. "I can't believe our first time together was against a tree," he chuckles ruefully and runs a hand through his hair as he pulls out of me. He ties the condom up. "We need a hidden stowaway place out here because I want to christen every inch of these woods."

I bend to pull on my clothes. "Nope," he nudges me forward and gestures behind him. "I'm giving you a piggyback ride back to the cabin."

"With no clothes?"

"Nope. Because we're not done. This is only the beginning of a very long night," he warns.

We didn't make it to the bed. We're sprawled on the couch where we collapsed after he made me bend over the arm. It feels warm and familiar, and I can't help remembering what it felt like to snuggle against him after he rescued me from the storm. The only difference is that we're completely naked now. In every way possible. I know his story and he knows almost all of mine. It's time to tell him the rest.

He yawns and stretches beneath me. It's sexy and perfect. Especially since I feel him rising against my thigh. He wraps his arms around me and pulls me into him. When I'm snuggled against his chest, he uses his fingers to untangle my hair, pushing it over my shoulder. "What were you thinking of just now?" he sleepily asks.

"I was trying to gather my courage to tell you things you deserve to know."

"I know something terrible happened to you, Fierce Girl. I know it's why you don't let your guard down with just anyone, and why you keep me at an emotional distance."

My breath whooshes out of my body. So he probably knows about the shooting. "I'm the reason my sister is dead," I confess. The confession sticks in my throat, burning my cheeks. I'm submerged in a tub of icy water, scrabbling against the sides to get out before I drown.

"I don't think that's true," he tips my chin up. "You can tell me the whole story because I think you need to tell it to someone who believes in you and your goodness. Someone who won't judge you for decisions you made and events you couldn't control."

He's giving me benediction. It flows over me, and the ice in my veins disappears. I can breathe again, and there's a lump in my throat for an entirely different reason.

"She came to see me at the afterparty. She couldn't get away from work to come to the game, so she left my twin nieces with her husband and showed up at the bar to support me," I exhale, marshaling my memories. "I'd been ignoring the stalker for months. I didn't take him seriously because the presents and messages were never violent, just creepy. I didn't know he was following me. When he pulled out the gun, I thought I was hallucinating. He was yelling at me, and I stood there, frozen. He opened fire and Beth shoved me down. In the aftermath, I didn't even realize she was gone. She was slumped against me, and I just thought she hit her head," my voice turns raw and I'm crying. "She got hit multiple times, and one of the bullets just stopped her heart. There was nothing the paramedics could do. If I'd reported this guy to the police he wouldn't have had the opportunity. She'd still be here. Now my nieces are without their mom," I sob. That was the thing that hurt the most. I knew she would have been an amazing mom. Kind and supportive and patient. Everything our mom wasn't. Because she was all those things to her much younger sister.

"You had no way of knowing he would show up with a gun. Especially since you'd seen no evidence of violent behavior," he rubs a soothing hand from my nape to the bottom of my spine. "And even if his behavior was creepy and you reported it and got a restraining order against him, the police still might not have been able to stop him."

I know he's only speaking the truth. I've tried to convince myself I'm not to blame. When you're constantly surrounded by people who look at you with nothing but accusation and disappointment, it's hard to forgive yourself. It's the reason I left my would-be fiancé and my almost wedding. "There's more I need to tell you," I murmur.

"Bring it, on, Sarah. Nothing you tell me is going to change the way I feel about you."

"I feel like an idiot," I confess. "That prick you met in the café duped me with his promise to make sure I never needed to worry about anything ever again. I didn't realize at the time that it was a cage. When I finally realized that I was running away from my fears and assuaging the mantle of guilt my parents laid on my shoulders, I climbed out the window."

"I can tell he's a master manipulator. You were afraid if you waited until the altar to leave he'd use your guilt against you and convince you to stay. And that would've meant you were more trapped than ever."

"Exactly. I was grieving for the one person in my life who accepted me as I am, and he took advantage of that."

"How did you two meet?"

"He's my brother-in-law's brother."

"Oh, wow," he says in disbelief. "That's complicated."

"Yeah. Part of the reason I accepted was because I felt this responsibility to my nieces to step in and be there for them. I'd convinced myself I didn't deserve to be anything other than a placeholder. Instead, I fled across the country, and I've missed everything. They don't even know me. They started kindergarten this year and they don't even know they have an aunt," this confession makes the tears fall again.

"That's not your fault. It sounds like everyone did everything they could to push you away, to ensure you had no other choice if you were going to keep yourself intact," he observes. "But you have a decision to make now that he's found you. What are you going to do, Sarah?"

He's right. I've been avoiding that outcome. I need to decide if I'm going to let people back in my life or move on without them. I know I'm never moving back there. Does that mean I'll never see my parents again? Or my nieces? Or their father, Alaric? If I mend the bridges between myself and my brother-in-law, if I become the aunt I always dreamed of being, even if it's long distance, how is my life going to change? "I need to make sure Ed knows that I am not going back with him. I need to make sure he knows that I'm making my life here."

"Do your parents know you're here?"

"I'm sure they do by now. He was always the perfect gentleman around them, and my mom could never stop talking about him."

"Is his brother the same way? What if he won't let you see your nieces?"

"I think Alaric will understand. He's the black sheep of the family – a nuclear physicist who turned his back on their wealth. He's with a lab at the University of Washington. He did what he could to get away too." I realize that Alaric will be the most understanding of my situation. That he's the one person I should've kept in contact with. Even though he's a brooding mess, my sister said he had a big gooey heart and that's why she was so crazy in love with him. She said they'd decided to live several hours away so they'd be able to carry on without the interference of parents. I could've talked to him about her.

"I think you should make it very clear to Ed you are taken," he pauses. "Otherwise, that may not be the last glimpse he gets of my fists."

"I'll make it very clear I'm staying, and I have no desire to pick up where we left off."

"Good," he rumbles. "And I think you need to reach out to your brother-in-law."

"I'm going to. I want to see my nieces. Beth would be so mad at me for staying away so long, for letting our parents' ridiculous expectations dictate my choices."

His encouragement just lifted a boulder from around my neck and I drift back to sleep in the circle of his arms.

Chapter 27

Blake

"So we're doing Secret Santa for Friendsgiving, except there's a twist." Zane informs me while grinning like a lunatic.

I've learned to brace myself whenever he tells me he's thought of a twist to something that should be pretty straightforward. "Okay…"

"You have to make something," he explains.

"That shouldn't be too hard."

"Speak for yourself," grunts Dex.

"I'm giving you three weeks to come up with something awesome. We're drawing names at dinner tonight and I expect the two of you to back up my bet with Taren."

"Of course you have a hidden agenda," I mutter.

"Not really hidden. I just want to prove to her that men can be just as creative as women."

"Are you sure that was a smart bet?" asks Dex.

"Yes, I'm sure. I know you guys won't let me down. I'm pretty sure Taren has the drawing rigged so we'll all draw the name we want. You need to kill it."

"So now we have extra pressure because not only do we have to bowl over the woman we're interested in, but also cement the reputation of our entire gender? Kill me now," complains Dex.

I lean over to bump fists with him. "My thoughts exactly, bro."

Zane just shakes his head at us. "You two have no imagination. You should be embracing this challenge like it's an invitation to attend Mortal Kombat or something."

"It's definitely something," scoffs Dex.

"Dude. This is your chance to shine and show the woman you love that you see her. If you ever want to earn her forgiveness for whatever the hell went down between the two of you, this is how you start. Like I said but let me re-emphasize --- Taren rigged it. Don't fuck up your shot to make it right."

Dex looks sheepish and disgruntled. "She has her reasons for hating the ground I walk on."

"Well change that. You can make her see that you're that grouchy lion with the thorn in its paw and you just need her to change your trajectory," Zane calmly berates him.

"I know Sarah's at least in it for the sex. I keep telling her I'm not going anywhere. I don't know if I've convinced her yet."

"Didn't you say she finally met Ellery?"

"Yeah, and they were both dogging me within five minutes."

Zane laughs. "That's what they do- keep us on our game. Ellery's coming to Friendsgiving, right?"

"She's so excited. She knows more about Willow Creek than I do because she googled the shit out of it and burrowed underneath like fifteen million rabbit warrens of information." I've talked about my little sister so much to these guys, I know they'll be like surrogate big brothers. We'll make sure she never dates someone unworthy.

Sarah's the unknown quantity. The sex is amazing because we're both adventurous and completely attuned to each other.

"Is Taren's brother coming?" I ask. I'm curious because I've never met him.

"Taren said he's actually moving back here. He got a job as a deputy at the county sheriff's office."

"I thought he went to Philadelphia because he was ready for a change?" Although I immediately recognized this town was exactly what I needed, Trevor was here his entire life. Maybe it wasn't what he needed.

"He did. Taren said he was disillusioned pretty quickly, that it wasn't what he thought it would be. She's trying to cook up something between him and Emma."

"Oh, wow. Emma with the bottomless pit of sarcasm and the reputation for squashing fragile male egos like grapes?" I ask in disbelief.

"Yep," he clarifies. "Apparently there's some unresolved tension."

"Please don't tell me that's another trope," Dex complains.

"Not technically, no. But best friend's brother is definitely a trope."

"Are you gonna try and make him join the romance book club too?" Dex sarcastically asks.

"It might be good for him. Even I can tell Emma isn't someone a guy can win over with the usual tricks in his arsenal."

"What if he doesn't want to win her over? Are you the town matchmaker now?"

Dex kind of has a point. Zane and Taren have this weird compulsion to sprinkle their in-love vibes over every single person in the entire town. They want their happiness to blanket everyone else too. I haven't vocalized how I feel, but I'm relatively certain I'm in love with Sarah. I've never felt this way about someone.

"I'd love to have a reputation as the town matchmaker. Like that old lady with the mustache from Mulan," Zane laughs.

"Next thing we know you're going to engineer a blizzard so you can make the snowed in trope a reality," I predict.

Zane's eyes light up. "If only I could control the weather or build a big enough snow machine. Maybe that's what it'll take for Marianela to finally give Dex the time of day."

Chapter 28

Sarah

I FIGURED THE CAFÉ was neutral ground. An audience is more likely, and that'll give me the courage to be very resolute when I talk to him. Edgar Vandervilt has rarely heard the word no. When he does hear it, he assumes it's an anomaly that he can easily remedy with charm or bribery.

I'm finished with my cupcake and my second cup of matcha, ready to leave, thankful I have one less confrontational person to deal with, when he strolls in twenty minutes late. He's glaring instead of smiling, his signature charm completely absent. Hopefully he recognizes it won't be any help.

"Sarah," he sneers as he slides into the booth across from me."

"Good morning, Ed."

"It's not a good morning. That motel bed was like a rock. Someone told me there was a bed and breakfast, but when I checked she told me she didn't have a vacancy for pond scum from Washington D.C."

I want to laugh hysterically and bite my lip to keep it from bubbling out. I wish Mrs. Snead had let him stay at Sweet Pea's. Maybe her demonic Persians would've sent him screaming all the way out of town. I still can't believe Blake lasted as long as he did. "A lot of small towns have characters like Mrs. Snead. If you're going to run for POTUS again you should grow a thicker skin," I comment.

"I don't need your advice on how to win an election. You've always been too much of an odd duck to be Miss Popularity."

"You just can't keep that streak of vicious hidden, can you?" I chide. I don't know how he ever had me so hoodwinked. My grief and guilt blinded me to his glaring faults, and I twisted myself into a miserable pretzel to fit into the role he designed for me.

"You're the only one who thinks so. I'm the most desirable bachelor in Washington," he smugly informs me, crossing his arms over his chest.

"And that's exactly why you belong there and not here."

"Come on, Sarah. You can't be serious about this nonsense. This isn't how you were raised. You have a responsibility to your family to make a certain kind of marriage."

"My family has a responsibility to me to want what's best for me. No matter what that looks like. Even if what I want is something they've never experienced and not the future they envisioned when they were planning out my life for me."

"So you're making your stand, then? You're going to wither away in the back of beyond like something dying on a vine?" He goads me.

"I'm not withering away. I'm spreading my wings."

"You're pathetic," he scoffs. "Chasing after that glorified grease monkey who grew up in foster care," he curls his lip in derision. "His millions will never erase his sordid background or the grime under his nails."

"He has more backbone in his pinky than you'll ever have in your entire body. It almost took me too long to realize what a sorry piece of shit for a human being you are. I want to smack my past self for ever letting you almost corral me into a life that horrifies me."

"You just burned your last bridge. Don't come crying to me when you get tired of this place," he snarls. He doesn't even bother saying goodbye. He just stomps away.

My ice cream date with Zane got derailed by the arrival of my ex, and I'm going to need an Oreo sundae after the call I know I need to make but am dreading with every ounce of my being.

It's the weekend, so they should be home. Ensconced in their living room catching up on their reading. I take a deep breath and dial; glad I didn't give into temptation and delete it.

It rings shrilly three times. And then someone picks up. "I don't recognize this number. Who is this?" my mother demands with a cool, precise tone.

"It's me, Mother."

I can almost hear her self-satisfied smile. "Ah, Sarah. I see that Edgar found you. When are you coming home to straighten out the mess you made? The debacle of your near wedding was the talk of our circle for a very long time."

"I'm not coming back."

She absorbs my statement. It's quiet and I know she's seething. "Well, Ed can't very well move there. He has a political career here and he has to maintain residency."

"I don't care where he goes."

"That's not how an affianced woman should behave, Sarah," she chastises.

"We're not affianced. And we never will be again," I retort. "I'm staying here in Willow Creek. I like living my life for myself."

"Well, you're making a mistake," she coldly replies. "You won't get a cent from your father and I. We've already written you out of our will."

"I don't care. I don't need your money. I never wanted it. The sacrifice isn't worth it."

"I should be accustomed to the disappointments you've rained down on our family your entire life," she crisply concludes.

"And that's exactly why I left and why I have no desire to return. Have a nice retirement, Mother and give my father my regards." I hang up before she can inject any more poison into the conversation.

The next call is one I don't dread as much. Alaric and I have always gotten along. And I know he barely tolerates his smarmy brother.

"Hi, Sarah," he answers on the first ring. "When my idiot brother told me he was going to bring you home, I knew you'd call me."

"Hi, Alaric. I'm sorry I haven't called. I'm sorry I missed so much."

He's quiet for a minute. "You have nothing to apologize for. We all needed to grieve in our own way. Including you. And no one should've held that against you."

"She was there because of me."

"Sarah, that's ridiculous. You know perfectly well that Beth wasn't going to do anything she didn't want to do. I miss her because she was the love of my life and the mother of my children, but I don't blame you for the fact that she's not here."

"Can I see the girls? I want to be a real aunt."

"Of course. We can visit you on spring break."

"I can come there."

"That would be awkward for you. And we always need a change of scenery. We'll see you in April. But I want more than that. You were the closest person to Beth, and I need someone to share memories with," he says tentatively.

"You can call me any time."

"I may take you up on that offer sooner than you think. You're a sister to me as much as you were to Beth, and I miss you. I want the girls to have you in their lives because you're the only person in either of our families who doesn't walk around thinking they're here to bless the minions with their presence."

I laugh self-consciously. It's sad that he's right. The three us were always stuck in a corner at family gatherings, observing the shenanigans and posturing with a sense of awe and disbelief.

"I appreciate it, Alaric. You're like a big brother to me and I'm sorry I didn't contact you sooner."

We agree to set up bi-weekly Facetime dates so I can get to know my nieces.

Chapter 29

Blake

I'M SURPRISED THE TABLE hasn't buckled under the weight of the Thanksgiving spread. There are at least nine different kinds of pies because Emma is making us try all her new holiday recipes. There's turkey and ham. There's mashed potatoes and okra and collard greens and green bean casserole. There's sweet potato souffle and ranch pasta salad. All the fixings you'd expect to find on a Southern menu.

Ellery is snugged between Sarah and I. She's looking at the food with a glazed expression. "Wow, dormitory food is going to taste like cardboard after this," she informs us.

Sarah laughs. "Maybe we can send you dessert care packages from Cupcake on Main."

"That'd be amazing! I'd be more popular than the girl whose mom sends her cake pops every semester."

She and Sarah hit it off more solidly in person than they did over Zoom. Ellery demolished us at Clue last night and made us take shots to redeem ourselves. Sarah didn't even bother walking back to her own cabin. It's fixed, but every day, I notice more of her in my space. Her toothbrush is in a glass jar over my sink. She has at least four scrunchies around the base of the lamp closest to the bed. Her favorite coffee mug hangs on the rack by the Keurig.

Of course I drew her name for the Secret Santa. Zane let me know that Taren didn't follow through with the rigging this time, that it was meant to be. I finished her gift after she fell asleep last night. We're exchanging them after we eat, and I'm excited and nervous at the same time.

Dinner is all bustling elbows and everyone sharing embarrassing anecdotes with Ellery about my life in Willow Creek. She shares some as well. I know it's because they care about me, so I just laugh along with everyone else.

Once everything's been scraped clean and loaded in the dishwasher, Zane motions for us all to gather in the living room. He and Taren put up an artificial tree yesterday, and the twinkling lights make the room seem even more homey and welcoming.

Sarah's nestled against me on the floor, her head against my shoulder. I told Zane I wanted to go last, and I wanted privacy, so as the master of ceremonies, he's obliging me. Almost all the gifts are baked goods. Except for Dex's. He drew Marianela's name and he carved and painted a candy skull for her to hang in the clinic. She seems stunned and nods her thanks. Maybe he's taking Zane's advice after all.

Emma isn't here and neither is Trevor. She had to leave town for some reason and because he's her police protection, he was hot on her heels, angry that she left without telling him.

It's finally my turn. "Okay, everyone out," Zane directs.

The package has glittery paper that looks like stars, and a silvery ribbon I thought looked like a sliver of moonlight. Ellery wrapped it for me and made me promise I'd let

Sarah know she was the one responsible for the impeccable presentation.

"Why'd everyone leave the room?" she nervously asks.

"Because there are things I need to say after you open my present and I told Zane I didn't want an audience. This is between you and me."

"Okay," she murmurs. "I find it hard to believe Ellery surrendered so easily."

I laugh. "She didn't. I let her wrap it in exchange. I'm glad I did because it looks way prettier than it would've if I'd been the one doing it."

She carefully removes the tape and slowly folds the tissue paper out of the way. Her eyes fill with tears when she sees the pink chenille. She lifts the hot pink crocheted cap to her face and strokes the mittens. "How did you remember?'

"I remember everything you say to me. It isn't from a window, but when you told me the story I heard how wistful you were. I wanted to show you I'll always listen."

"It reminds me of Phoebe's bonnet from the window," she tearfully confesses.

"That's what I wanted it to remind you of. You told me that's what you wanted. To be seen." I take a deep breath. "I see you. I've seen you from the very first moment. Even the things you try to hide. I'm crazy in love with you. I'm staying here in Willow Creek because of all the reasons I told you I was ready to find somewhere to belong. But I have someone I want to belong to as well."

She reaches over and clasps my hand. "I want to belong to you, too. You make me feel safe when I feel my anxiety creeping up on me. You're strong, yet vulnerable. You're wise and protective and make me feel invincible. I've fallen in love with you."

I lift her face to mine. "Please say you'll move onto the farm with me when it's ready," I plead.

"Yes," she closes her eyes and rests her forehead against mine.

The kiss consumes us. It's a promise of togetherness, of having someone at your back to help you fight your battles and bring you hot tea when you need it. It's the promise of being snuggled in a blanket beneath the stars, and days spent fishing on the lake.

It's not surrendering, it's coming full circle.

We break apart when our friends come bursting through the door. They're all clapping and happy for us, and the world is telling me again this is where I'm meant to be.

Acknowledgments

I'm ever grateful to my beta reader besties, Rue and Whitney, and my ARC team. I'm grateful to all of the wonderful romance authors who've been there to support my writing journey and have been nothing but graceful and encouraging – especially Janna Macgregor and Julie Anne Long.

As always, none of this would be possible if I didn't have an amazing spouse who reminds me every day what true love is all about. Anthony, you have all my love, forever.

Meet the Author

Andrea has been reading romance since she stole her aunt's copy of Ashes in the Wind at the age of twelve. She's a dreamer at heart who believes in seeing the good in people and crafting characters and stories that will resonate with readers.

She loves Reese Cups, dark beer (especially porters and stouts), is happiest in leggings, boots, flannel and a baseball cap, and can ramble on for hours about anything. She lives on a farm with her husband and believes that small towns doesn't mean small minds. She daydreams on her porch swing about one day bottling her own cider and perry. No Surrender is the second book in her Willow Creek series. All of the books in the series are set in the small town of

Willow Creek, but can be read as standalones because they each feature the love story of a different couple.